MARTIN McLean, Middle School QUEEN

MARTIN McLean, Middle School QUEEN

BY ALYSSA ZACZEK

STERLING CHILDREN'S BOOKS
New York

STERLING CHILDREN'S BOOKS
New York

An Imprint of Sterling Publishing Co., Inc.
1166 Avenue of the Americas
New York, NY 10036

ISBN 978-1-4549-3570-4

Library of Congress Cataloging-in-Publication Data
Names: Zaczek, Alyssa, author.
Title: Martin McLean, middle school queen / by Alyssa Zaczek.
Description: New York : Sterling, [2020] | Summary: Seventh-grader Martin McLean has trouble expressing himself except at Mathletes competitions and now, as a female impersonator but his first-ever drag show falls on the same night as an important Mathletes tournament.
Identifiers: LCCN 2019018074 | ISBN 9781454935704 (book / hc_plc with jacket)
Subjects: | CYAC: Female impersonators—Fiction. |
  Mathematics—Competitions—Fiction. | Best friends—Fiction. |
  Friendship—Fiction. | Junior high schools—Fiction. | Schools—Fiction. |
  Single-parent families—Fiction. | Hispanic Americans—Fiction.
Classification: LCC PZ7.1.Z26 Mar 2020 | DDC [Fic]—dc23 2019018074
LC record available at https://lccn.loc.gov/2019018074

Distributed in Canada by Sterling Publishing Co., Inc.
c/o Canadian Manda Group, 664 Annette Street
Toronto, Ontario M6S 2C8, Canada
Distributed in the United Kingdom by GMC Distribution Services
Castle Place, 166 High Street, Lewes, East Sussex BN7 1XU, England
Distributed in Australia by NewSouth Books
University of New South Wales, Sydney, NSW 2052, Australia

For information about custom editions, special sales, and premium and corporate purchases, please contact Sterling Special Sales at 800-805-5489 or specialsales@sterlingpublishing.com.

Manufactured in Canada

Lot #:
2 4 6 8 10 9 7 5 3 1
12/19

sterlingpublishing.com

Cover and interior design by Irene Vandervoort

For little **Alyssa**,
who never gave up on big **Alyssa**

SEPTEMBER

☆ 1 ☆

I hadn't seen either of my best friends all summer, and I was so bored, time felt like it was moving backward. Carmen had been off with her mom on an architectural tour of Italy, and Pickle spent every summer with his elderly aunt on her farm. Frankly, I thought the summer apart took a much harder toll on me than it did on them. Sure, we kept in contact, but while they were off paddling gondolas and raising barns, I was forced to watch *Property Brothers* reruns with Mom for three months ("Ay, mira que rico they both are!").

When she wasn't swooning over reality TV stars, Mom spent the summer telling me I needed to work on "expressing myself." That was easy for her to say. Mom's an artist, and she was *always* creating. Her latest thing? A tropical-themed mural on our living room wall—a gigantic portrait of her whole family—which, of course, included me. I couldn't help but wonder if the whole "expression" kick was her way of trying to force me to fit into her world. Mom's world, the one of paint and color and '80s dance music, is for people who like being center stage. My world is for people who would rather be in the audience. It's a small world, my world, but I like it that way. I've found that being quiet is much safer than being loud.

Maybe that's why Pickle, Carmen, and I work so well together. We've been a package deal ever since we met in third grade. Mom calls them parlanchines—chatterboxes—and when I can't find the right words, they *always* have something to say.

Obviously, then, the first day of seventh grade was especially exciting, because I finally had my best friends back.

After lunch, we grabbed some prime real estate near the stairwell in the seventh-grade hallway to wait out the passing period.

"I *haaaaate* this," Carmen moaned, slumping against the lockers. "Being on a different floor than last year sucks. My locker is on the other side of the building! I'll never make it to the vending machines *and* get to drama rehearsal on time."

"Consider yourself lucky," Pickle said. "I can't even reach my top shelves."

"You couldn't do that before."

"Well, you don't have to rub it in."

Carmen Miranda was named after the singer with fruit on her head, even though her parents are Mexican, not Brazilian. She's the giggliest person I've ever met, and she's big in every sense of the word, right down to her personality. She has a gap between her two front teeth, and it makes her smile especially wide and pretty. I think some people get tired of Carmen because she never takes anything seriously, but I like that she has a sense of humor.

And Pickle is . . . well, he's Pickle. His real name is Peter, but everyone has always called him Pickle, and no one really knows why. It could be because Pickle is generally pretty sour—Mom says he's "self-deprecating," always making fun of himself. He and Carmen get along because he cracks jokes about himself and she laughs, and that just makes him tell more. Pickle says he has a lot to joke about because he's at least a whole foot shorter than most everybody in our class, and his ears stick out so far that sometimes he compares them to the handlebars of a bicycle. But I think Pickle really makes fun of himself so other people don't do it first.

"You think Rafferty's gonna make us play floor hockey again this year?" Carmen asked, changing the subject. She shuffled her brightly colored notebooks against her chest. "That was so miserable."

"Better than the pickleball unit. The jokes that

Charlie Chaudhari made. . . " Pickle shuddered.

"I heard they're going to incorporate a dance unit," I said. Actually, dance didn't sound so bad to me. As much as I hated the thought of our whole class staring at me while I stumbled through a box step with some poor unsuspecting girl, at least there'd be no running involved. I don't run unless someone is chasing me.

Just then, a pretty, dark-haired girl passed us in the hall and waved to us from her motorized wheelchair. Pickle turned the color of a cherry paleta. "H-hi, Violet," Pickle stammered, raising a hand. Violet beamed and turned her chair toward us, meeting us by the lockers. I heard Pickle gulp from three feet away. Carmen giggled, delighted by his discomfort. Violet Levi is the girl that Pickle is massively, hopelessly in love with. She's the first chair clarinetist in the school band, which is how Pickle got to know her. (He plays percussion; you should see him try to look at his music stand with a bass drum strapped to his chest.) It's true that Violet is pretty—she has warm eyes and her hair, sleek and black, is the longest of anyone in our grade—but I think Pickle likes her because she's basically the nicest person in Bloomington. She has never, ever made fun of his height, not even once.

Her adoptive parents, the Levis, named her Violet when they brought her home from Vietnam, and she *loves* her name. Like, *really* loves it. She color-coordinates everything she owns to it, including her wheelchair: various shades of purple, plum, lavender, and, of course, violet. Privately, Carmen and I find this to be a little eccentric. Pickle finds it adorable.

"Hey, you three!" Violet beamed. "Did you have a good summer?"

"It was okay," I shrugged. "I read a lot of comics."

"I saw the most amazing theater in Italy," Carmen said with a wistful sigh. "Did you know they, like, *invented* masked theater? I mean, the Greeks started it and all, but the Italians basically made it go viral. Even if it was, like, the 1500s."

"Cool!" Violet said, nodding appreciatively. "I went to sleepaway band camp in Indianapolis. We played a bunch of music by Italian composers. I bet you would have liked it!" She turned her gaze on Pickle, who looked as though he was about to melt into the ground. "Did you do anything fun?"

"I, uh, um—I—well, so, um—I—farm? Farm. Farm," Pickle spluttered. Carmen stifled a screech of laughter, perilously close to hysterics. Violet wrinkled her nose in confusion. "Farm?" Pickle repeated, looking at me with panic in his eyes.

"You . . . were on a farm?" Violet asked, glancing at Carmen and me for clarification. I blanched; poor Pickle.

"Yes!" I jumped in. "Yes. He was on a farm with his aunt. He actually helped build a barn. With his bare hands! Right, Pickle?"

Pickle nodded vigorously, and I swore I saw a bead of sweat form on his forehead. Violet's smile returned, her braces laced tight with purple rubber bands. "Wow!" she said. "That's amazing. I wish I could have seen it!" The one minute–warning bell buzzed overhead, startling Pickle so badly he jumped. "Oops, gotta head to English. We'll have to catch up more later. See you in band!" Violet said, looking directly at Pickle. He whimpered.

"Ooh," Carmen cooed at Pickle as Violet motored off. "I bet she would love to see you in gym, sambaing away!"

"Shut up," he hissed. "I'm not dancing with anybody."

"Violet wouldn't be in gym class anyway," I said. "She's got an exemption." Violet was born a paraplegic, which means she can't use her legs and feet to walk.

"See?" Pickle said triumphantly. "Your dastardly plans are foiled, thou wicked woman." He wriggled his fingers toward Carmen, who rolled her eyes.

"I never said you had to dance *with* Violet. Don't be such a drama queen," she said. Pickle gasped and pretended to clutch his chest in deep offense. "Come on, we're going to be late for math."

I had been looking forward to Mr. Peterson's class, for three reasons.

1. Math is my best subject.
2. Mr. Peterson coaches Junior Mathletes and therefore likes me.

3. It's the only class that Carmen, Pickle, and I have together, besides lunch.

All three of us sat in the front of the room by virtue of assigned seating. The downside to math class is that Nelson Turlington sat with us too.

"Well, if it isn't Gordita Supreme and her two amigos," Nelson sneered as we filtered into class. Carmen's face grew blotchy with anger.

"Bite me, Turlington," she said, her fists clenched.

"Sorry, my mom has me on a low-fat diet."

"I'm surprised she has the energy to plan your meals. She must be exhausted from picking out all your outfits too," Pickle shot back. Nelson's upper lip curled. The problem with Nelson is that his parents are very rich and he is very handsome. I think this is something that probably plagues a lot of bullies. When you're tall and tan and blonde, and your teeth are straight and your clothes are new and your hair isn't coily, you can get away with a lot. Nelson seemed to be very aware of that.

"Awfully protective of the Chiquita Banana today, Pickle," he observed. Nelson leaned back precariously in his chair. "I wonder if Violet has some competition?"

"Mind your business, Nelson," I mumbled, settling into my desk. A strange, smug smile stretched across his mouth. He raised an eyebrow at me.

"Huh," he said, "maybe she really *does* have some competition." Before I could open my mouth to respond, the bell rang, and Mr. Peterson began walking toward the Smartboard at the front of the class.

"What does he mean?" Carmen whispered.

"Forget it," I said, shaking my head. "It's just Nelson being Nelson."

Carmen stifled a tiny snort, but Nelson's words echoed in my head. *Maybe she really does have some competition.* What *did* that mean? Did Nelson think I had a crush? On Pickle? Mr. Peterson passed around a syllabus and gestured to the board. *Nelson doesn't know what he's talking about. Pickle likes Violet. Pickle likes girls. I like girls.*

I think.

I hesitate to admit this, but in the interest of "expression" I think I should be honest. I've never actually had a crush on a girl before. Not ever. I mean, I like girls the way I like Carmen, but I've never *like*-liked a girl.

Does that make me weird? Everyone else seems to have had hundreds of crushes by now, but how can I really know what's normal? *Is* there such a thing? It's not as though the guys in my grade get together and discuss girls. Pickle's the exception, but that's different, because he only talks to Carmen and me and he only talks about one girl in particular. And Mom has definitely never talked to me about crushes or when it's okay to like girls or any of that. I know some stuff thanks to the internet, but beyond that, nobody's ever told me if not like-liking girls by now is normal.

And if I don't like-like girls, does that automatically mean I like boys? Are those the only options? That makes me really anxious. Meadow Crest Junior High is a lot of things, but particularly accepting it is not. Back in fourth grade, when we were at Bloomington Elementary, Pickle and Carmen and I heard a story about a kid who came out as gay in eighth grade. They said he ended up having to switch schools because nobody would sit with him at lunch and people kept stealing his uniform during gym. I heard that someone beat him up at recess, too, but I don't know if that's true or not. It might all be an urban legend, but still: is that the fate that awaits me if I never have a crush on a girl? And how am I supposed to figure out who I am, when everyone else around me seems to know without having to ask themselves the question?

"Martin?" Mr. Peterson's voice bore down on me, snapping me back to reality. "Are you still with us?"

"Huh?"

I looked up at him in surprise. Mr. Peterson is pretty young for a teacher, and he looks like an owl that was put through Willy Wonka's taffy puller: all lanky limbs and long nose with horn-rimmed glasses and big eyes. He wears his lucky tweed jacket on the first day of school every year and also at the final Junior Mathletes competition every season. I found myself staring at his elbow patches as I struggled to remember the last thing he said.

"I asked if anyone in the class could define the Pythagorean theorem," he said, pushing his glasses up to the bridge of his nose. He gestured widely to the class. No one had raised their hand. "I thought you might be able to help us out."

"Me? N-no," I replied, still shaking myself out of my thoughts. Mr. Peterson stared hard at me.

"No? That's odd," he said, "seeing how you helped the Mathletes take second place at Regionals last year using it." He crossed his arms over his chest, waiting. Across from me, Pickle winced and put his head down on his desk.

"Dude," he groaned. "Embarrassing."

"Uh. Oh!" I stammered at Mr. Peterson. "The Pythagorean theorem. *That* Pythagorean theorem. Right. Um. It's $a^2+b^2=c^2$. The square of the hypotenuse of a right triangle is equal to the sum of the squares of the two other sides."

"Very good," Mr. Peterson said. He gave me a small smile before returning to the board. "I'm glad to see your lapse in memory was temporary. Chalk it up to the first day of school, yes?"

Still dazed, I didn't answer. Carmen was giggling into her hand while Pickle tried to shush her. As

Mr. Peterson continued the lesson, Nelson leaned over and whispered in my ear.

"Romantic daydreams, McLean?" Nelson snickered under his breath. "McLean the Queen. That has a ring to it, doesn't it?"

My stomach dropped, then turned sour. My heart picked up in my chest, beating like it was trying to stage a prison break—*tha-RUMP tha-RUMP tha-RUMP.* I watched Carmen doodle stars in her notebook until my eyes glazed over, willing that distraction to drown out the thrumming in my ears. *What is happening?* Everything around me sounded as though I were underwater. Time had stopped moving. I realized I had doubled over like I had been punched in the gut. My throat was tight, and the air wasn't getting to my lungs fast enough. I leapt up out of my chair, knocking it over with a metallic *CLANG*—

And then it was just the pounding in my ears—

And the lights that were too bright—

And the silence that was too loud—

And—

tha-RUMP tha-RUMP tha-RUMP.

Every face in the room stared at me, blank and surprised—

tha-RUMP tha-RUMP tha-RUMP.

And I ran.

I just ran. My legs made the choice themselves,

backing out of the room and scrambling out the door in one flash of movement. When my brain finally caught up with my body, I was halfway down the hall, gasping for breath. I put my hands on my knees and let my head hang. *Great. Awesome start to the school year. Now everybody thinks I had botched brain surgery over summer vacation.*

I sank to the floor, leaning my back against a bay of lockers. I closed my eyes, listening to my heartbeat slow. *What was that?*

"Martin?" I heard Mr. Peterson's voice from down the hall. The sinking weight of embarrassment settled heavily in the pit of my stomach. I buried my face beneath my arms, my elbows resting on my knees. Mr. Peterson's footsteps grew closer. He knelt down and tentatively put a hand on my shoulder. "Is everything all right?"

Obviously not.

I nodded into my arms without looking up. There was a shuffling and jumbling of long limbs, and when I shifted my head to peek out, I found Mr. Peterson sitting next to me. He peered down at me from behind his thick glasses, his brows knit together in a worried frown.

"I'm okay," I said to the floor. "I . . . don't know why I did that."

"I know you're a perfectionist, Martin, but believe me, everyone zones out in class from time to time. Even straight-A students like you," he replied.

The voice inside me wanted so badly to tell Mr. Peterson about what Nelson said to me, about how it made me feel sad and scared in a way I couldn't put my finger on. I wanted to tell Mr. Peterson, but I didn't. Instead I nodded solemnly.

"I know."

"Okay," Mr. Peterson said. He took off his glasses and polished them with the corner of his plaid shirt. "Martin," he said, blinking as he placed the glasses back on his nose, "have you had panic attacks like this before?"

It was my turn to blink.

"This wasn't a panic attack," I said.

Mr. Peterson gave me a kind, gentle smile. "Sometimes," he said slowly, "these things can sneak up on us. Especially the first time. Sometimes we don't even know what's happening to us until it's over. The feelings—and the physical response that comes with them—can seem to come out of nowhere. It can be overwhelming and even a little frightening."

A look of recognition appeared on Mr. Peterson's face, and I realized I was nodding. "That's okay," he continued. "It's nothing to be ashamed of. Lots of people have what are called 'triggers.' Triggers are experiences or topics or images that cause someone to have a fight-or-flight response, just like you did."

"Fight-or-flight?" I asked, wrinkling my nose. "I thought cavemen used that to figure out their chances of survival against mammoths and stuff."

"That's true," Mr. Peterson said. "But you'd be surprised what holdovers from bygone eras still hang out in our DNA and in our brains. You had an emotional response, and your body interpreted it the way a caveman's body would have interpreted, say, an attack by a saber-toothed tiger."

"That's weird," I said.

"That's science."

"But you're a math teacher, Mr. Peterson."

Mr. Peterson laughed, a full-body guffaw that sent his head backward against the lockers. I smiled to myself, just a little.

"I'm sorry I left class," I said. "I didn't mean to."

"You don't have to apologize, Martin," he said. "If anything, I'm sorry if my putting you on the spot contributed to this experience at all."

"It wasn't that," I said, not meeting his gaze.

"Do you want to—"

But the bell rang, and Mr. Peterson didn't have the chance to finish. Instead he clapped me on the shoulder and helped me up. Kids started pouring out of their classrooms, and I was blissfully freed from having to slink back into Math to face everyone.

Do you want to talk about it? No, Mr. Peterson, I really don't. Even if I could find the words, I wasn't about to tell him that it wasn't a teaching tactic that turned me into the Road Runner, it was the thought of Nelson spreading around the rumor that I like boys.

Because I don't like boys. Right?

★ ★ ★

LadyOfTheStage: Soooo…?

mathletesmartin: So, what?

LadyOfTheStage: So, how are you?

mathletesmartin: Swell

LadyOfTheStage: Martin!

mathletesmartin: What?!

LadyOfTheStage: Uh, the last time we saw you, you were Usain Bolt-ing out of Peterson's class. You totally avoided us for rest of the day!

PicknLittle: Dude, what WAS that?

mathletesmartin: I will pay you each $5 to stop asking me that question.

PicknLittle: Make it $10

PicknLittle: And then we have a deal

LadyOfTheStage: Seriously, are you okay?

mathletesmartin: $10 it is!

LadyOfTheStage: Fiiiiine

PicknLittle: Yessss

mathletesmartin: Lovely as always, Pickle!

LadyOfTheStage: Hey Martin, when does Mathletes practice start back up?

mathletesmartin: Tomorrow

LadyOfTheStage: And that's only on weekdays, right?

mathletesmartin: Unless we have a tournament

LadyOfTheStage: Do you have one this weekend?

mathletesmartin: Nope. Why?

LadyOfTheStage: No reason

LadyOfTheStage: Pickle, are you doing that Dungeons & Dragons club at the gaming store again this year?

PicknLittle: I believe I'll be gracing the realm with my gnome bard's presence, yes.

LadyOfTheStage: And that starts…?

PicknLittle: This Sunday. What are you up to?

mathletesmartin: I do not like the sound of this

LadyOfTheStage: Don't be so paranoid!

PicknLittle: Spill it, lady

LadyOfTheStage: I'm sure I haven't the slightest idea what you're talking about.

mathletesmartin: Carmen, whatever you're planning, we're about 5000 times more likely to go along with it if you just tell us.

PicknLittle: Truly. Out with it!

LadyOfTheStage: Fiiiiiine, ruin the surprise if you must.

LadyOfTheStage: So, I talked to Violet today…

PicknLittle: DID SHE SAY ANYTHING ABOUT ME???

mathletesmartin: Dude

LadyOfTheStage: WAIT AND SEE, WHY DON'T YOU

PicknLittle: FINE.

LadyOfTheStage: FINE. ANYWAY.

mathletesmartin: Go on…

LadyOfTheStage: I talked to Violet today and I asked her what she's doing this weekend.

LadyOfTheStage: Turns out she's free, so I invited her to go bowling with us!

PicknLittle: !!!!!!

LadyOfTheStage: What do you think?

PicknLittle: !!!!!!!!!!!!!!!!!!!!!!!!!!!!!!!!!!!!

mathletesmartin: I think you've killed Pickle.

LadyOfTheStage: He had it comin'

mathletesmartin: *Chicago*, nice!

LadyOfTheStage: Thank you! Loooove me some Kander & Ebb.

PicknLittle: I can't see her!

mathletesmartin: What are you talking about?

PicknLittle: I'm not ready!

mathletesmartin: You see her every day at school!

PicknLittle: That's different!

LadyOfTheStage: How?!

PicknLittle: That's, you know, school!

PicknLittle: I've never hung out with her outside of school!

PicknLittle: I need her to think I'm cool and collected and date-worthy, not all unprepared and doofusy!

mathletesmartin: It's not really a date, though

PicknLittle: But it could be the first step toward a date

LadyOfTheStage: If she thought you were a doofus, she wouldn't have agreed to come.

mathletesmartin: That's true!

PicknLittle: You did tell her I would be there, right?

LadyOfTheStage: Yes, obviously!

PicknLittle: Okay

PicknLittle: Now I need you to describe her exact facial expression upon hearing my name.

LadyOfTheStage: Oh, she swooned. Physically swooned.

LadyOfTheStage: Hand fluttered to her forehead, eyes rolled back in her head, knees buckling, the whole bit.

PicknLittle: Really?!

mathletesmartin: Oh my God

LadyOfTheStage: No, not really!

PicknLittle: Don't tease me! I'm a man in love!

LadyOfTheStage: Are you coming or not?

PicknLittle: Martin?

mathletesmartin: Totally up to you, dude. It's your future marriage at stake.

PicknLittle: Don't say such things, you'll give me a heart attack.

PicknLittle: Okay. Okay!

PicknLittle: Yeah

PicknLittle: Yes

PicknLittle: I'll go

LadyOfTheStage: Finally. Good! I'll text her and

let her know we're all in.

PicknLittle: I can't believe I'm going to hang out with Violet Levi this weekend.

PicknLittle: I'm going to need my inhaler.

LadyOfTheStage: We're going to meet at Bloomington Bowl at 6 on Saturday night, okay?

PicknLittle: My palms are clammy just thinking about this.

LadyOfTheStage: Maybe don't say stuff like that to Violet. That's not awesome first date talk.

PicknLittle: YOU SAID IT WASN'T REALLY A DATE

LadyOfTheStage: Well!

PicknLittle: I have to go pick an outfit. What do you think she'd like me in?

mathletesmartin: Nothing orange, you'll clash

LadyOfTheStage: Maybe something purple?

PicknLittle: Very funny, you two

ReadMe App
SEPT. 4—5:12 P.M.

LadyOfTheStage: Martin! It's totally a date!

mathletesmartin: What do you mean? We'll both be there with them.

LadyOfTheStage: Actually…

mathletesmartin: ?!

LadyOfTheStage: It would be oh-so-convenient if we both, say, had last-minute conflicts that night.

mathletesmartin: Pickle is going to kill you!

LadyOfTheStage: No, he won't

LadyOfTheStage: He'll be far too busy having a romantic night under the DayGlo stars during cosmic bowling.

mathletesmartin: Man, last year's production of *Hello, Dolly!* really did a number on you.

LadyOfTheStage: Hey, Martin?

mathletesmartin: Hey, Carmen?

LadyOfTheStage: Are you really okay?

mathletesmartin: Yeah. I am.

LadyOfTheStage: Good. Because if someone made you feel not-okay, I'd kick them in the shins.

mathletesmartin: Yikes

LadyOfTheStage: In my character shoes

mathletesmartin: Double yikes

LadyOfTheStage: Promise you're okay?

mathletesmartin: Super-duper, double-dog, mega-extra promise

LadyOfTheStage: With sprinkles on top?

mathletesmartin: With sprinkles on top

LadyOfTheStage: Well, okay then! Shoot. Now I'm hungry. Wanna go get ice cream?

☆ 2 ☆

"**M**ijo! What happened?"

Mom pounced on me in the living room as soon as I got home, pacing the floor in her bare feet and the denim overalls she wears to paint. I inherited her dark corkscrew curls, but her Afro-Cuban brownness mixed with my dad's Irish blood, and I came out looking more cafe con leche than cafecito. Still, I have her warm hazel eyes, which were particularly wide as she anxiously guided me to the couch.

"Mr. Peterson told you?" I asked. She nodded, and I watched a fuchsia paint smudge on her cheek bounce up and down. "It was really nothing, Mom."

"Don't lie to me," she wagged her finger. "I didn't raise you to lie to me."

"I'm not lying!"

"Then qué pasó, Martín?" she asked, pronouncing

my name the Spanish way. She always did that when she got upset.

"I don't know. I was daydreaming in class and Mr. Peterson took me by surprise, that's all," I said. "It was totally weird, and it'll never happen again."

Honestly, I hadn't even expected her to be home—she almost never is. Teaching eats up most of her time; it doesn't pay a ton, so she has to take on a lot of classes to pay the bills. I spend a lot of afternoons home alone, heating up Easy Mac and reading comics while she's in class or rubbing elbows at galleries.

"And what if it does, huh?"

I shrugged. I couldn't think about it happening again, because the first time was embarrassing enough. Mom ran a hand through her hair and leaned back against our couch, which is beige and lumpy and covered in ridiculous pillows. Some of these were gifts from Mom's artist friends and have dirty sayings on them.

"Baby, you can talk to me," she said. She took my hands in hers, warm but rough from constant washing in the big painter's sink in her backyard studio. "What can I do?"

I didn't know what to say, which is admittedly not a new phenomenon for me. But what was I supposed to tell her? *Hi Mom, today I had an episode at school because the class bully implied I like boys!*

But don't worry, I'm just totally freaked out and completely confused.

No way.

"I'm fine," I said. "I just want to forget about it." At least that part was true.

"Espérate. Uh-uh. We have to talk this out," she said in her Don't Mess With Me voice. I groaned.

"Mom—"

"It's important for you to communicate your feelings," she said, wrapping her arms around a throw pillow. "Tell me, what were you doing when it happened?"

"Just sitting in class, I don't know!" I said, getting annoyed. Mom always does this. She tries to make up for never being around by laying the Textbook Parenting on thick when she actually *is* here. Sometimes I'd give just about anything for her to talk to me like I'm a person.

"Well, you must know."

"I don't!" I gestured wildly, exasperated. "It just *happened* to me!"

Mom's expression softened. She patted the spot on the couch next to her. I sighed and hesitantly scooched closer. She put an arm around me and rested her chin on the top of my head.

"Is this my fault?" she said after a moment, so quietly I could barely hear her. I pulled back slightly to face her, and her eyes were studying me as though she had never seen me before. "Did I do something to make you—I mean, if you have anxiety, was it something I did? Is it not having your dad around?"

"Mom, no, no way," I said. But I wasn't totally sure that was true. You hear all the time on the news and in movies and stuff about how not having a father can mess a person up. I didn't know if that's what happened to me, but I knew Dad leaving didn't help, at least in the "expression" department.

"I would hate to think that maybe because of the way I raised you, you're suffering now."

"I'm not suffering. Honest."

"There's nothing wrong with feeling your feelings, baby," she said. "I want you to know that. I know you're probably embarrassed by what happened today, but that's okay. You're okay." Mom kissed my forehead, and then looked at me very seriously. "You have to promise me that you'll talk to me. About anything, anything under the sun. That's my job, baby. Can you do that for me? Can you promise?"

You don't know how much I can't do that, Mom, I thought. But instead I nodded.

It's not that I don't think Mom would understand. It's more that *I* don't understand. And I can't promise to tell anyone anything, because half the time I can't even find the words to explain the things inside my own head. If whatever happened to me in Mr. Peterson's class was just some passing weirdness, then it's not worth getting into with Mom. She'd have all kinds of questions—questions that I doubt I could answer—and she'd want to talk it out. I'm not so great at talking it out. I have things I want to say, of course, important things; it's more that when I open my mouth to say them, nothing comes out.

With Mom satisfied, I slipped upstairs to my room. It's no Fortress of Solitude or Stark Tower, but it does the trick when I want to be alone, which is pretty often. I've got my gaming systems and TV set up in one corner, and my games are organized alphabetically by title on the shelves beneath my window seat.

But I think my favorite part of my personal Inner Sanctum is my constellations. When I turn off the lights, glow-in-the-dark stars radiate a weak greenish light above me. Every night I lie in bed and stare at them, imagining all the planets and galaxies out there in the dark beyond and what might live on them, and it soothes me right to sleep.

After talking to Mom, I didn't feel like sleeping or gaming or even reading comics, so I queued up some music videos on YouTube. Mom raised me on all sorts of weird music, from Scottish folk to salsa to '80s hair bands. My favorite singers are Celia Cruz and David Bowie. I love Celia's voice most of all, but I love Bowie because of his colorful outfits and his hair, especially in that old movie *Labyrinth*. Mom and I sometimes quote it back and forth. She likes it because all the goblins look like cute Muppets, and I like it for all the singing and dancing.

But Bowie and his hilariously tight pants aside, my favorite video is Celia Cruz singing "Yo Viviré" in some grainy footage ripped from an old primetime cable broadcast. The music is actually the same as "I Will Survive," the famous Gloria Gaynor song, but Celia's lyrics are totally different. Personally, I think the song is a thousand times better Celia's way. In this footage, Celia is wearing this fabulous sequined, beaded jacket and a magenta bob with bangs, and during the instrumental breaks she busts out some salsa steps, despite being in her sixties or seventies at the time. She's so glamorous, and when she looks at the camera it's as though she's singing just to me. Her music makes me feel like I could do anything, be anyone—maybe even someone who can find the words to stand up to a bully or tell his mom what he's feeling.

Eventually I turned the music way down and set it to loop, so I could get ready for bed. I've always liked a little white noise when I settle in for the night. The sound of heavy rain outside sends me right to sleep. Mom says Dad liked the sound of rain too; that he splurged on an expensive machine that made all kinds of soothing noises to help him sleep. I wonder if he still has that. I wonder if he ever thinks of me before he goes to bed at night.

It's not as though I live every day like: *I'm*

pouring cereal, and my dad isn't here. I'm on the bus, and my dad isn't here. I'm at the dentist, and my dad isn't here. But I do think about him. I wonder what he's doing and whether he ever wonders about me. Mom works so hard for us, but it can be lonely, and sometimes when I come home to an empty house after school, I wish he were there. I wish I had someone to help me with my homework, or to cook me dinner, or to split the chores with me. And that's complicated, because it feels strange to miss a dad I never really knew, who never really wanted to know me. Does he ever think about me when he's tucking his new kids into bed at night?

I settled in and looked up at the plastic stars on my ceiling glowing away. I put them up after a field trip to the planetarium a few years ago. It was on that trip that I learned astronomers use math to chart the stars and even propel people into space. Math turns into physics, which turns into astronomy, which turns into astrophysics engineering. And although most of that is a little out of my league right now, someday I'll understand it all. I want to be an astronomer and use what I know to make miracles happen, like putting real live people on Mars. And then I'll come back to Bloomington and talk to seventh graders just like me, and explain to them that everything, everything in the whole universe, boils down to numbers: simple, logical, solvable.

I wish everything were that simple. When

Carmen or Mom asks me to promise that I'll talk to them, they make it sound so easy. But a promise is complicated. A promise is something you're not supposed to break. And promising to talk about my feelings seems risky, because I can break it without ever opening my mouth. Sure, a promise seems simple on the outside, but on the inside, I felt like a galaxy on the farthest edge of space, hurtling faster and faster as the universe grows forever outward, sending it spinning into the dark unknown.

★ ★ ★

I spent the next day at school silently worried someone would ask me about my freak-out in Mr. Peterson's class, but no one ever did. Not even Nelson, though it turned out he was saving his insults for Junior Mathletes.

We had our first practice after school in Mr. Peterson's room. As soon as I walked in, I was immediately at ease. Mathletes is my favorite thing on the planet. I get to flex my math skills *and* win things, all without saying a word. Well, sometimes I have to read our answers aloud, but those are just numbers, and I'm almost always correct. Mostly, it's writing down your work and hitting a buzzer, like on *Jeopardy*, and that's just enough interaction for me.

The whole team is expected to have a working knowledge of all the testing sections during a competition, but we all have our preferences. Ironically, mine are word problems. Together, the seven of us function sort of like one of those sitcom families. We bicker (a lot) but when push comes to shove, we actually make a pretty good team. When Nelson isn't oozing everywhere, that is.

"I think I should be team captain," he announced over cookies and lemonade. He was chewing with his mouth open, arms tucked behind his head and feet up on his desk like some kind of charmless Calvin Klein model. "It just makes sense."

"*How* does that make sense, exactly?" Mariam Khan rolled her eyes as she brushed hot pink crumbs off her burgundy hijab.

"Yeah, technically, Chris and I have seniority," John-Paul Cregg said, cocking his head toward his twin brother. "Eighth graders, yo."

"We can't have co-captains." Poppy Liu looked up from her sketchbook, frowning. Her shiny black bangs flopped into her brown eyes. "The whole point of having a captain is that there's only one."

"Exactly, and it should be me," Nelson said.

"Support your thesis," I said, trying to be diplomatic. The rest of the team nodded. Nelson blinked for a moment.

"Well," he stammered, "I'm—I'm obviously the most handsome, for starters."

Everyone groaned.

"You're so full of it," Poppy said.

"I think you like it."

"Gag me."

"Anyone else have any nominations?" Konrad Kozlowski asked.

"Bearing in mind that co-captains are not an option," Poppy added.

"Says who?"

"Says logic, J.P."

"What are you, a Vulcan now? What's the prime directive, Poppy?"

"You realize in using that insult, you're outing yourself as a Trekkie, right?"

"You say that like it's a bad thing."

"What about Martin?"

The din of conversation was cut abruptly short. Everyone turned to look at Christopher-Jack Cregg, who had been totally quiet up to that point. Although Chris and J.P. have the same face—long and spotted with freckles and dark moles—and are both super popular, Chris was always distinguishable in the pair as more of an introvert. Now, his brother stared at him in astonishment.

"Dude," he hissed at Chris, "we were actually getting somewhere. Martin?"

"Yeah," Chris said, as though it was the most obvious thing in the world. "He totally saved us at qualifiers last year. After *you* froze in the third round"— he pointed to Nelson, who turned pale—"Martin got us back in the game during sudden death."

"That was pretty cool," Mariam said, turning her heavily lined eyes on me approvingly.

"Totally cool," Chris confirmed.

"He's a seventh grader!" Nelson snarled.

"So are you!"

"But—but—that's not the point."

"You brought it up!"

"Guys," I interrupted, "this is really nice and all, but what if I don't want to be captain?"

"Why not?" Mariam asked.

"You're definitely smart enough," Konrad said. He would know; he's in Mensa and goes to all kinds of summer camps for genius kids. He's also the kind of pale that's almost translucent, partially because he is very, very Polish and partially because he has zero interest in any outdoor activities. I'm surprised he doesn't want to be captain himself, to be honest, but I bet he's too busy with all the tutoring he does on the side. He's probably going to run the world one day, or become a super villain. Either way, bright future.

"And we know you can lead drills and stuff," Mariam said. "You filled in for Angelica at our practices last year after she moved away."

"I know," I said, "but being captain means giving a speech if we win."

"So?" Chris asked.

"So . . . I don't do so well with public speaking."

"I don't believe you," Poppy said imperiously. "You always do fine on the podium."

"That's answering math questions, though," I explained. "I know those answers. And I'm not addressing a crowd of people, I'm addressing a math problem."

"So just write the speech down," J.P. suggested.

"Beginning to come around to the idea, huh?" Mariam flashed a coy smile at him.

"Quit flirting," Nelson said, and Mariam turned the color of her hijab. "If McLean has stage fright, he should be ineligible."

"I *don't*," I said. "I just . . . being team captain is a big job. I want to make sure I can do it well." Actually, being captain was all I had ever wanted for my junior high career, but being actually offered the job—as a seventh grader!—had suddenly turned my insides to Jell-O.

"I'm sure you will, Martin," Mr. Peterson said as he came sailing into the room with a freshly copied stack of schedules in his hands. "I see you've all selected a captain. Good choice. Let's get started."

I couldn't think of a thing to say (big surprise) but inside, I was beaming. As nervous as it made me, being voted captain of Junior Mathletes was a huge honor, and taking it on filled me with pride. I practically floated through Mr. Peterson's overview of the calendar, completely absorbed in visions of the team and me accepting our trophies at Regionals, confetti streaming from the ceiling as we smile and wave to the adoring crowd.

Of course, in reality, Regionals is held at the Baker's Lake Academy auditorium, which always smells faintly of burnt rubber, and the audience there tends to be pretty mild-mannered. But it's still a great fantasy, even if it would mean facing a big crowd. *I could be remembered forever as one of the greatest captains in the history of our team. I could even go on to a second term!* Victory was so close, I could taste it.

It tasted suspiciously like grocery store brand sugar cookies, actually.

☆ 3 ☆

When I got home from Mathletes practice the next Monday, an unfamiliar car was parked in the driveway. I hopped off my bike to roll it into the garage, and then I saw the plates on the car: Florida. That could only mean one thing.

"Tío Billy!" I cried as I threw open the door. I let my backpack slump to the floor and went flying into the living room.

"Hey, león, you gonna come and give your favorite tío a firm handshake?" My uncle Billy stood up from the couch with a big grin. Tall, tan, and slender, Tío Billy was the most fashionable person I knew. He was always wearing the latest trend, topped off with his signature slim, gray leather jacket. Between his outfits, his shiny, dark curls, and his dimpled Tom Cruise chin, he was definitely the most handsome member of our family.

"How do you know you're my favorite tío?" I

teased. Tío Billy stuck out his hand, and we did our secret handshake. We painstakingly developed it when I was seven. It's a slide and a wiggle, with a fist bump and a nod.

"Ay, very funny! You know, you're my only sobrino, so it's a good thing you're my favorite!" he said.

"What are you doing here?" I asked. Tío Billy lives in Florida with his husband. Uncle Isaiah is from Louisiana by way of Kenya, so he has the coolest accent. We don't see my uncles very often, because they're so busy running their theater group, but I always love it when we do.

Before Tío Billy could answer, Mom poked her head out of the kitchen.

"Hey, you two, dinner's ready!" She had her hair tied back with a wide, colorful bandana in shades of red and orange. She wiped her hands on her apron, and it occurred to me that I couldn't remember the last time she cooked a homemade meal.

Tío Billy and I headed into the kitchen, where Mom had laid out all my favorites: ropa vieja, arroz con frijoles, and maduros, sweet fried plantains. I even spied a tres leches cake sitting out on the counter in anticipation of dessert.

"Wow," I said, marveling at the full table. "Am I dying?"

"Oh, mijo," Mom said, half scolding. "I need a special occasion to cook for you now? Siéntate, the food is getting cold!"

"Better listen, león," Tío Billy whispered in my ear, loud enough for Mom to overhear. "My big sister wields a mean wooden spoon when she's mad." I giggled. Tío Billy has called me león—lion—since I was a baby because, as he tells it, all my wailing sounded like a little lion cub learning to roar. Mom said grace in Spanish, which she only ever does on the holidays, then we tucked into the food. I loaded up my plate with fried plantains, which are my absolute favorite, and a big heap of ropa vieja.

"So, seventh grade, huh?" Tío Billy asked, dishing out some rice. "How's the first week been?"

"Pretty good," I said around a mouthful of shredded beef. Then I realized I never told Mom about my big captain-of-the-Mathletes news. It's not that I didn't want to tell her, it's just that I didn't really have the chance. She was so wrapped up in classes starting again at the university that I was lucky if I saw her before I went to bed.

I opened up my mouth to tell them both, but Mom cleared her throat before I could.

"So, Martín," she began, "you're probably wondering why your tío Billy is here."

I swallowed a gulp of juice. Why was Mom using her Serious Business voice?

"I mean, I guess," I hedged. It *was* a little weird, but then, Tío Billy had always been the spontaneous type.

"I thought it might be good for him to stay with us for a bit," she said.

"Why? Did something happen?"

"No," Mom replied, shooting a weird look at Tío Billy. "Not exactly. For one thing, Tío Billy is on his way up to Chicago."

"How come?"

"Your Uncle Isaiah got a job there," Tío Billy said in his rumbly, good-natured voice. "He's going to be the artistic director of a big-deal children's theater company."

"Wow!" I said. "Tell him congrats for me."

"We're in the process of moving up there, but he went before me," Tío Billy continued. "You know, to get the apartment settled. He knows I don't carry boxes!" He smiled, and Mom snorted out a little laugh.

"You? No way. You'd always just sit around como una reina while the rest of us packed up!"

I giggled, and so did Tío Billy.

"*Anyway*," he said pointedly, brushing Mom off with a little wave of his fingers. "I figured I'd visit you two troublemakers and crash with you for a bit while Uncle Isaiah sets up our new pad."

Mom smiled, but her lips were pressed together hard, so I knew there was something more.

"I also thought . . ." Mom's eyes met mine, and for a second, she looked sad. "I thought maybe it might be good for you to have some male influence."

"Male influence?"

"Somebody to look up to," she explained. "Somebody to, I don't know, confide in. About guy stuff."

"Guy stuff?" I asked. I felt as if my brain had gone offline; I could only repeat the ends of her sentences. Mom never cared much about "guy stuff" before. Neither had I, if I'm being honest.

"You know, school and Mathletes, and any questions you might have about—"

Oh, no. "Don't say it!" I winced, but Mom was going full steam ahead.

"—puberty, and crushes, and all that," she said. "You know, cosas de hombres."

I groaned. Mom had always been insecure about raising me without a dad. How could I be sure Tío Billy was actually on his way to Chicago? Mom could have dragged him up here just to be a "male influence" on me. Or what if this was just a new, inventive excuse for her to not be around?

"Mom, I swear, I don't have any questions," I said, putting down my knife and fork. "I'm fine. Really!"

"You need to talk about your feelings, mijo! I don't like this, all this panicking at school and bottling yourself up," she exclaimed. "You're almost a teenager now, and it must feel like there are things I wouldn't understand, right? So, that's what

Tío Billy is here for!" Mom gestured to him. "If you ever feel like you can't talk to me—even though you absolutely can, baby—you can talk to him!"

"I don't want to talk at all," I said. "I don't have anything to talk *about*."

"Well, that's okay too!" Mom said brightly. "You can talk about whatever you want, it doesn't have to be anything big."

"We can hang, right, leoncito? No pressure?" Tío Billy said.

"I just don't understand where this is coming from," I said, shaking my head. "Am I being punished for something?"

"Punished?" Mom asked, incredulous.

"Well, you ordered me up a babysitter," I said, feeling the frustration rise in my gut. I looked at Tío Billy. "I'm really glad to see you and everything, but I don't need any 'male influence.'"

"I thought—" Mom began, then dabbed at her eyes with her napkin. "After your . . . incident at school, I thought maybe you'd feel more comfortable with your emotions if you had someone in your life that you could relate to," she said. "Another guy, you know. To help you talk through things." She sighed, her breath ragged. "I know I'm not around very much, Martín," she said, suddenly very serious, "but you know I love you more than anything. I just want you to thrive!"

My head was swimming, and for a moment I felt

just like I had in math class that day. I stood up from the dinner table abruptly, shoving my chair away.

"Martín?" Mom said, looking surprised.

I don't . . ." I struggled to figure out what to say. "I'm . . . Tío Billy, I'm really sorry she made you drive all the way up here for me, but I'm fine. I don't need to be 'influenced,' or whatever." The more the words spilled out, the angrier I got, and then I couldn't stop.

"I'm sorry I'm not like you!" I yelled, turning my gaze on Mom, who was sitting with her hands folded in her lap. Suddenly she looked like a scared, sad little kid, but it was too late. "Sorry I don't vocalize every single thought or feeling that has ever passed through my head! Some of us like to think before we speak! I don't know why that's such a bad thing!"

"Baby," Mom said. Her cheeks were stained with tears and her nose was red.

"No, okay? I'm fine. I'm fine by myself. I'm pretty used to that by now. I don't need Tío Billy to teach me how to be a man, because I've been the only guy in this house since Dad left!"

Mom looked as though my words had physically hit her. *And* this *is why I never speak my mind. It never comes out the way I want it to.*

Tío Billy started to stand up from the table and come over to me, but tears were brimming in my eyes and a lump rising in my throat, so I threw my napkin down on my plate and ran off as fast as I could.

Halfway upstairs, I realized I never told them my news, and that somehow made me even angrier. I stopped mid-stair.

"And by the way," I yelled, "I'm captain of the Mathletes!"

And then I pounded up to my room and slammed the door.

I landed face down in my bed, feeling so awful I could puke. I've never raised my voice to Mom before. Not once. Not ever. I swore I'd never do that after hearing Dad scream at her over and over again before the divorce. And now I'd gone and made her cry, and probably Tío Billy, too, all in one night. I planted my face firmly into my pillow.

She was just trying to do something nice. She didn't mean to offend me, she just wants me to be happy. I felt hot tears sneak out of the corners of my eyes. I had been a jerk. A huge, massive jerk.

I wiped my nose on the back of my hand and sat up, trying to catch my breath. I could hear Mom and Tío Billy's muffled voices talking at the bottom of the stairs. I got off my bed and tiptoed to the door, cracking it open just enough to hear what they were saying.

"I don't know what's going on with him," Mom said. I could picture her pacing and wringing her hands. "Do I go up there?"

"Let him be," Tío Billy said, his low voice carrying upward. "He needs a little space." I heard Mom sniffle, and then a pause—I think they were hugging. "He didn't mean what he said, Gena. He was just upset and surprised."

"I thought he'd *like* the surprise," Mom said, her voice thick. "I thought he'd be happy to see you."

"He was, mana, but we also caught him off guard," Tío Billy said. "Remember how I was at his age? Everything was the end of the world. He'll be all right once he cools down. Just give him some time. C'mon."

Their footsteps disappeared, rounding the corner back into the kitchen. I closed my door carefully, so it wouldn't squeak, then slumped to the ground with my back against it. The terrible feeling of having upset Mom was eating away at my insides.

Eventually I scraped myself off the floor and shuffled over to my telescope. My dad got it for me for my birthday—well, the last birthday he was here for, six years ago. I never got to use it with him. It's not fancy or anything and its tech is pretty old at this point, but it does the job. Sometimes I look through it at night and pretend that I'm already a famous astronomer, searching the sky for signs of alien life or new galaxies hundreds of light years away. I haven't found anything like that yet, but maybe someday I will.

That night, it didn't seem like there was much

going on out there in the universe. The skies were clear and calm; I didn't even see any planes overhead. But I know better than to think that outer space is boring or uneventful. No matter how quiet things are on the surface, there's always something incredible happening beyond that, even if we can't see it. Even on the stillest of nights, somewhere out there, there are storms brewing on distant planets, galaxies colliding, stars exploding into being, so far away from Earth that we don't even have the words to describe it. It's comforting to me to think that even the smartest scientists in the world sometimes can't find the right words.

I took notes on the position and visibility of Saturn and Jupiter and Mars, and eventually, I calmed down. I changed into my pajamas, my favorite button-down set with Captain America shields all over it. My body felt achy from crying and my eyes sort of stung, but I did feel more clear-headed. Just as I was thinking about going downstairs and apologizing to Mom and Tío Billy, there was a gentle knock on the door.

"Come in," I called, but no one did, so I went and opened the door myself. There was no one there and no sign of anyone either—no one on the stairs or in the living room. But then I looked down, and at my feet was a plate with a big slice of tres leches cake and a full glass of milk. I peered down the hall toward Tío Billy's room and Mom's room, trying to see if anyone was watching me. I didn't see anyone, so I picked up the cake and the milk and retreated into my room, closing the door behind me with my foot.

I settled into bed with my cake, slicing a fork through the dessert's moist layers. As I chewed, something occurred to me that hadn't before: *Tío Billy likes boys.*

I mean, of course I knew Tío Billy liked boys; he's married to Uncle Isaiah. But I realized maybe the reason Mom called Tío Billy after my panic attack wasn't because he's a boy, like me—it's because he *likes* boys.

Like me?

The cake turned to heavy mush in my mouth. If I did like boys . . . would that be so bad?

Mom always says I can talk to her about anything. And I would, if I ever figured out what I wanted to say and how to say it. But how could I do that when I didn't even know where I stood? And if I did try to talk it through with Mom, there's no doubt she'd share *all* her opinions on the subject, which might make me more confused!

This is un gran desastre, I thought. *Maybe tomorrow, I can apologize. Maybe I can explain it all to Tío Billy instead. Maybe he'd understand if I told him about what Nelson said and how it made me feel. Maybe he could help, if I could get up the courage to ask.*

I took a deep breath, then another bite of tres leches. There were a lot of maybes ahead of me—I would *definitely* need more cake.

★ ★ ★

ReadMe App
SEPT. 11—5:39 PM

PicknLittle: TRAITORS
PicknLittle: VILLAINS
PicknLittle: SCOUNDRELS
LadyOfTheStage: ???
PicknLittle: DESERTERS
LadyOfTheStage: Ohhh, right, your bowling date! How'd that go?
mathletesmartin: It was Carmen's idea!
LadyOfTheStage: Hey!
mathletesmartin: It's true!
PicknLittle: I CANNOT BELIEVE
mathletesmartin: I'm so sorry, I swear I never meant to let her go through with this!
LadyOfTheStage: Double hey!
mathletesmartin: I just got distracted. My uncle is here visiting.
mathletesmartin: It was a bad idea, Pickle, I'm super sorry.
LadyOfTheStage: Woooooow
LadyOfTheStage: I'm doing just fine, beneath the

wheels of this bus you threw me under, thanks for asking.

mathletesmartin: Where were you today?

PicknLittle: I stayed home out of sheer embarrassment.

LadyOfTheStage: You're kidding

PicknLittle: I told my Mom I had a fever, but really I've been doused in flop sweat since Saturday night.

mathletesmartin: That bad, huh?

PicknLittle: I slipped.

LadyOfTheStage: No.

PicknLittle: On the lane

mathletesmartin: Oh, jeez

PicknLittle: Flat on my back, in front of God and Violet and everybody.

LadyOfTheStage: What did you DO?!

PicknLittle: After I determined that burrowing directly into the ground would take too much time?

PicknLittle: I stood up and pretended it was a bit

mathletesmartin: Oh, *jeez*

PicknLittle: You know, a Three Stooges sort of thing

PicknLittle: Pratfalls, and whatnot

mathletesmartin: If you say you turned to prop comedy next, I'm logging off.

LadyOfTheStage: What did she say?!

LadyOfTheStage: Was she totally mortified for you?

LadyOfTheStage: Did she leave?

PicknLittle: She…giggled.

LadyOfTheStage: She laughed at you?! That witch!

PicknLittle: No, no, like, she...giggled.

mathletesmartin: Like...a cute giggle?

LadyOfTheStage: Like a she-thought-YOU-were-cute giggle?

PicknLittle: Exactly like that.

LadyOfTheStage: !!!!!!

mathletesmartin: Oh my God. Pickle's met his soulmate.

PicknLittle: So I'm not imagining things? You think she could actually like me?!

LadyOfTheStage: Okay, I will have to hear an EXACT replication of this giggle, plus a play-by-play dramatic reenactment of the following conversation, immediately upon seeing you tomorrow. We'll work from there.

PicknLittle: When she scored a strike, she let me spin her around.

PicknLittle: I mean, technically she was doing the spinning, because she controls her wheelchair and all. But I was holding her hand!

PicknLittle: HOLDING HER HAND, YOU GUYS

mathletesmartin: That's the most adorable thing I've ever heard.

LadyOfTheStage: Sooo...I guess you could say we did you a favor in the end?

PicknLittle: Not a chance, woman, you're still on my list.

LadyOfTheStage: Drat.

☆ 4 ☆

Tío Billy burst into my room late Saturday afternoon with a huge smile on his face. We hadn't spoken much since his first night here—a whole five days earlier, which felt like a lifetime—but now there he was, coaxing me out of my beanbag chair and up onto my feet.

"Vamos, león!" he trilled, tossing me my coat. "Come on! Throw some clothes on and meet me downstairs in five."

"Where are we going?" I asked, but he just waved his hands as he sailed out of the room. I changed out of my grubby sweats and into a pair of jeans and a T-shirt as fast as I could. Then I bounded down the stairs to the living room and found Mom working on her mural, painting orange flowers over one of the last blank spaces on the wall. Things between us had been tense since the big blowup— I still couldn't figure out the right way to apologize—

but when she looked up from her work, she smiled.

"Hey, mijo," she said, wiping her hands on her overalls. "Tío Billy's taking you out, huh?"

"Do you know where we're going?"

"You'll have to ask him!" she replied with a playful wink.

"I already did! He wouldn't say."

"Then I guess you'll have to wait and see," Tío Billy said from the doorway, still grinning. "Come on, we've got a schedule to keep!"

"Chao pescao," Mom said, kissing my cheek with a wet smack of her lips.

"Y a la vuelta picadillo!" I answered, heading out the door.

I was vibrating with excitement as I scurried into Tío Billy's car. He's always up to something when he visits us: surprise trips to the zoo, sneaking me out for late-night movies with tons of candy, or putting Mom's paintbrushes in the freezer just to hear her curse him out in Spanish. Whatever he was planning, it was bound to be good.

Eventually we turned onto Kirkwood in downtown Bloomington, which was teeming with people milling about, heading to the restaurants and bars. Bloomington is a college town, so there's lots of young people and their families, but since Indiana University is a Big Ten school, most of them are rich, preppy white people. Tío Billy pulled into a parking lot set off from a coffee shop, and we hopped out of the car. Looking around, there were white college students in their cream and crimson, sure, but also a group of Japanese students with massive carryout cups and some young Black men and women reading under one of the umbrellas.

I had walked by the place before with Pickle and Carmen on our way to Hartzell's for scoops of Moose Tracks (Pickle), bubblegum (Carmen), and Cookie Monster (me), but I'd never really paid attention to it before. The exterior appeared more or less like an old Victorian-style house, with a porch and a garden, though the roof was done up in white twinkle lights with a big rainbow flag pinned up on the overhang. In the front yard, a glossy white sign read "HOOSIER MAMA? COFFEE HOUSE" in bubbly retro-style letters.

"A coffee house?" I asked. "You know Mom keeps plenty of coffee at home, right?"

Tío Billy laughed as we strolled up the pathway. "C'mon," he said. "I want you to meet some of my friends."

"You have friends in Indiana?"

Tío Billy gave me a quizzical look.

"Hey, your tío used to be a big deal on this campus! I know people!" He pretended to be miffed, but I giggled, and sure enough, he threw me our secret handshake. After the last nod was completed, he swung open the front door and ushered me inside.

The smell of just-roasted coffee and baked goods filled the air, enveloping us like a warm hug. Big chalkboard signs with wacky cartoon illustrations showed off the daily specials, and a massive fish tank filled with tropical fish and a lone glitter roller skate separated the counter area from the seating. Overstuffed chairs and mismatched couches sat on intricate woven rugs against walls covered almost completely with weird art, from oil portraits of Russian generals to vivid spray-paint pop art to a cerulean bust of a ram wearing a beret.

"Whoa," I whispered. Tío Billy's hand lifted from my shoulder, and he swept past me to embrace a short Black woman.

"Hey, Dorie!" Tío Billy was smiling warmly as he wrapped his long arms around the woman. "Miss me?"

"You wish! What, you're too good for us now, Mr. Miami?" The woman pulled out of the embrace to look Tío Billy up and down. Her long, dark locs were secured on top of her head with iridescent chopsticks, and she was wearing glasses with huge black frames. Beneath her white apron, which was stained a little with what looked like strawberry jam, she had on a "Save the Daleks" T-shirt and a gray tweed vest with jeans. She swatted at Tío Billy with a tea towel. "You look exactly the same. How is that possible? Who did you sell your soul to, and what's the going rate, huh?"

"You should talk!" Tío Billy laughed. "You haven't changed a bit. But what—excuse my French—the *hell* are those?" He gestured to the woman's feet, upon which she wore sandal-like slide-on shoes that featured a strange cap over the toes.

"Custom Birkenstocks. Gotta have closed-toe shoes for kitchen work, but I didn't want to sacrifice my classic look, so . . ." She wiggled her toes for emphasis. "You like 'em?"

"Oh, no, I'm not taking that bait! I know better than to comment on your fashion choices," Tío Billy said. "Hey, I've got someone I want you to meet. Dorie, this is Martin McLean. Martin, Dorie owns this place and is an old friend of mine."

"Excuse you," Dorie said, wrinkling her nose. "Speak for yourself when you're calling people old!" She laughed, a big, boisterous belly chuckle. "It's good to meet you, Martin. Any friend of Billy's is a friend of mine."

"Martin's my nephew," Tío Billy added as I shyly shook Dorie's hand. "He's been a little down lately." He met my eye, and I felt sorry all over again that I had yelled at him and Mom. "I thought he might like to see the show tonight," he continued.

"Sure," Dorie said. "Ever been to a show before?" Confused, I shook my head. *A show?* She grinned. "You're in for a treat. Make yourself comfortable downstairs. Billy, show him where to be. Can I get you anything while you wait?"

And that's how I ended up in the basement of Hoosier Mama sipping hot chocolate out of a mug with "WORLD'S BEST BIG SISTER" printed on it in big block letters. Tío Billy came downstairs with me, steered me toward one of the folding chairs that faced the stage, and then disappeared somewhere. The basement area was the same long shape as the upstairs, with a big elevator in one corner. The stage, which looked like it was probably built by hand, took up most of the back wall and even stretched out into the room a little, like a runway. A black curtain obscured the backstage from view, and a disco ball hung overhead, spinning lazily.

I wasn't sure what I was supposed to be waiting for, but as I drank my hot chocolate, people started to trickle into the room from upstairs. They began filling the rows, some of them hanging back near a sound booth that had funky dance music playing. The crowd was mostly men, with a smattering of women. There were college students in baseball caps and shorts, and older men in button-downs and slacks. Some of the men wore eyeliner, glitter, and lipstick, while others wore beards instead of makeup, or nothing on their faces at all. Some hung out together in big huddles, while others seemed to flit from group to group. Everyone was laughing and talking, hollering hello to people they knew over the heads of people they didn't, wrapping their friends in massive hugs or showering them with kisses.

I had never seen so many different types of people before in my life, let alone all in one room. My class was pretty diverse, but I was the only mixed kid I knew, and that made it so easy to feel out of place. I could never totally relate to the white kids, but I couldn't totally relate to the other Latinos either. Where was I supposed to fit in?

Now, suddenly, I was in a room with people of all shapes, sizes, and colors, and I felt . . . at home. Everyone was hanging out together: people of every race, every gender, and all different styles of dress. I saw a skinny, mixed-looking college guy wearing lime green short shorts and a mesh shirt chatting up a man with glitter in his beard, his mustache twirled into fancy curlicues. A man in a Lucky Brand T-shirt and jeans held the hand of the bearded man. A woman with the biggest Afro I'd ever seen winked at me as she passed by, handing a steaming mug of tea to a pale woman with a shaved head and an ear (and eyebrow!) full of piercings. All the while, people were dancing to the music that was pumping out of the speakers. It was as though a big party and an art installation had a loud Technicolor baby.

As I took in all the excitement, I saw Dorie slip behind the sound booth. After a moment, the music lowered to a hum, and Dorie's voice rang out from over the speakers, deep and rich like my hot chocolate.

"Ladies and gentlemen and everyone in

between! Thank you all for coming tonight to our Bargain Basement Babes drag show!" A cheer, some applause, and a couple peals of laughter rose up from the crowd, which had begun to settle into the seats around me. Behind her huge frames, Dorie's eyes sparkled when she spoke. I had heard of drag shows before but never seen one. I knew from the internet that drag queens were men who dressed up as women, but I had no idea what a drag show might be like or why Tío Billy would bring me here.

"I know we do this show every Saturday, but tonight is a special one. We've got Cassie Blanca in the house tonight!" More applause, and someone whooped loudly in the crowd. "It's been many, many moons since she's graced our stage, but don't ask her *how* many, 'cause a lady's real age is between herself and God—and her plastic surgeon!" Dorie kept talking over the laughter. "Anyway, I hope you enjoy tonight's show. And if afterward you find yourself longing for more, you can catch me as Ewan Dangergirl at next week's Kings and Queens–themed night. Now, are you ready for our first performer?"

Dorie held out her microphone, and the crowd cheered as colorful lights danced, bouncing off the disco ball in the center of the ceiling. "She's our haute homemaker, our own big-boned Betty Draper; she is . . . Aida Lott!"

When the clapping subsided, there was a beat of silence that reverberated with anticipation. The curtains parted, the lights came up on stage, and at the center stood a vision in blonde curls and polka dots.

And then: she started singing, and I was entranced.

Her cherry red lips were moving along to the music, but then . . . *Wait,* I realized, *she's not actually singing.* She was lip-syncing, but with so much conviction, it was as if it were her own song. As if she were the only singer who had ever sung anything, ever, in the history of time and space. She was *that* confident. She didn't actually have to say a single thing—she was telling us how she felt with her movement, her smile, her expression.

It was dazzling. It was magic. It was magnetic.

The bass thrummed in my chest—*tha-RUMP tha-RUMP tha-RUMP.* My heart was pounding, just like in Math, but this time, it wasn't because I wanted to run away. I wanted to run *toward* the stage and climb up there with Aida, if it meant I could have even an ounce of her confidence.

I watched her in a blur of glitter and music and applause, the music swirling around me like a spell. Aida tore off her dress in one smooth, impossible motion to reveal a polka dot bikini. Then she fell into the splits, and I cheered along with the crowd. I didn't even think about it. I didn't worry about looking silly or what other people might think. I just whooped with excitement, as people leapt to their feet and rushed the stage with dollar bills in hand. Aida warmly accepted the cash and tucked it all into her bikini top with a wink and an air kiss.

My cocoa had gone cold, but I didn't care. I was dizzy from the energy in the room. By the time Aida took her final bow, I was dazed. Every atom in me was buzzing. *That. Was. Amazing.*

Dorie announced the next performer, then the next, giving each a funny little nickname or catchphrase. Dream Haus, a wisp of a blonde in a pink latex dress, "contains plastic parts, some assembly *is* required," according to Dorie. Billie Holligay was "The Sinful Songstress."

"There's a heat wave coming from the South," Dorie said as The Weather Girl, a queen with comically overblown makeup and an umbrella hat, took the stage. Laughing at her hilarious performance, I realized I hadn't stopped smiling yet. *My face hurts,* I thought, *and I love it.*

Then Dorie's voice came over the speakers with the enthusiasm of a fútbol announcer. "And now, it's time for our special guest this evening: the one, the only . . . Cassie Blanca!"

The crowd went bonkers at the name. Slowly, the curtain parted, revealing a tall, slender performer in a tan trench coat. She dangled a long cigarette holder between her fingers. Her face was obscured in the shadow cast by her matching fedora. A jazzy piano solo began to slink into the room over the speakers, and when Cassie Blanca tilted her head into the light, everyone started cheering—

And I gasped.

"Tío Billy!"

His face was painted to look like an old-school starlet in black and white, and his hair was covered by a curly half-black, half-white wig, but there was no mistaking: Tío Billy was Cassie Blanca.

No one heard me exclaim over all the applause as he slid out of his trench coat. He revealed a black and white suit with a skirt, the kind with shoulder pads and harsh lines I've seen Lois Lane wear in really old Superman comics. With a fabulous turn, he dropped the coat to the floor, and the beat dropped too, transforming the jazz piano into house music with a smoky swing. He bent his knees deep and bounced to the music, doing big movements with his hands and pouting elegantly.

This whole time, Tío Billy has had a whole other life, I thought, my mouth hanging open. *A secret identity. Like a superhero.* And he—she?—looked like one, spinning and strutting around the stage, hands on her hips. If Aida was confident, Cassie Blanca was the Grand Empress of Planet Confidence and All Its Inhabitants.

Tío Billy had always been that way (Mom calls him creído—conceited—even to his face sometimes!), but as Cassie he seemed . . . more. More himself, more self-assured, *more.* As Cassie, he was telling a different story about himself, a story that couldn't be told with a bare face and street clothes. The outfits, the hair, the makeup—it unleashed the real Tío Billy somehow. Cassie Blanca knew exactly who she was and what she was about, and she didn't care if you liked her or not. And she was Tío Billy, of all people!

At the end of the number, she caught my eye and winked at me, batting thick black lashes in my direction. The guys next to me cheered and ribbed me with their elbows. Cassie Blanca took her bow, and when the crowd stood, Dorie must have pressed a button from the sound booth, because glittering confetti came raining down from little pods on the ceiling that had opened up like Christmas crackers. Cassie Blanca laughed and took another bow, tossing her wig into the air. She looked so happy—and everyone else did too.

And all at once, I understood. I understood the cheering crowds and the giddy wave that swept over me as I watched the queens perform. I understood the feeling of family that radiated throughout the room. And I understood why Tío Billy brought me to the show: Because he knew I needed it.

"Why didn't you *tell* me?" I cried as he came out from backstage in his street clothes after the show.

"I thought showing you would be even better," he said, a big smile on his face. "What did you think?"

"It was amazing! Where did you learn to do that?"

"I started in college," Tío Billy said, shrugging. "I had done musical theater before, so I knew my way around a song-and-dance number. Well, more the song than the dance, but still. And theater kids are always looking for an excuse to perform."

"And you were no exception!" I heard Dorie's voice from behind me. She put an arm around me. "I take it you enjoyed yourself?"

I nodded wildly, not caring that my eyes were probably wild with excitement.

"Yes," I said. "I didn't even know you did this here. I mean, I didn't know there were drag queens in Bloomington."

"He also didn't know there were drag queens in his *family*," Tío Billy said wryly. Dorie burst into a wonderful, distinct laugh.

"Oh, Lord," she said, catching her breath. "They say you never forget your first show; I think for Martin here that might be doubly true."

"No doubt," Tío Billy agreed, ruffling my hair. "Thanks for having me out on such short notice, Dorie."

"Girl, please. You're a godsend. I've been having trouble packing the house lately, but a last-minute appearance by Miss Cassie Blanca seemed to do the trick. Everyone lost their minds when I posted about it," she said. "I just hope we can keep up that kind of interest."

"You know, I'll be in town for a little while," Tío

Billy said slowly. "Probably through the first of the year . . ."

"You're kidding!" Dorie exclaimed. "We'd love to have you anytime. Seriously, Billy, you'd be doing me a favor. I'm trying to drum up as much excitement as I can in advance of our big All-Ages Night."

"Yeah?" Billy asked. "Is that a new one?"

Dorie nodded. "We've got a lot of college kids who want to come out, plus some old timers looking to bust out their stilettos one last time. Bloomington's queer scene is as active as ever, but in order to keep the crowds coming, I've mostly been booking professionals. Better-known names bring in more folks—"

"Which means more ticket sales. I get it," Tío Billy said, putting an arm on Dorie's shoulder. "We have the same problem putting on shows in Miami. Everyone wants the done-to-death musicals; nobody wants to see a brand-new play."

"Exactly," Dorie said, with a sigh. "I've been saying for years that I want to book more amateurs, and All-Ages Night is our first step in doing that."

"It sounds great, Dorie," Tío Billy said. "I'm happy to help however I can."

"Keep bringing Cassie Blanca through my door, and we'll be in good shape!" Dorie laughed. "Gotta make that cash so I can offer our big All-Ages Night prize. We're gonna give the winner a thousand bucks."

"Wow," Tío Billy said, nodding in approval. "You're serious."

"Seriously serious," Dorie said. "Anyway, we've got time, the show isn't until January 27th. That's a couple of months' worth of begging people to buy tickets, right?"

"It's going to go fabulously," Tío Billy said, pulling Dorie into a hug. "I'll be in touch about booking, okay?"

"I'm going to hold you to that," Dorie said, wagging her finger at Tío Billy. Then she turned to me and hugged me tight against her chest. She smelled like a warm gingerbread latte. "You keep an eye on this uncle of yours, okay, Martin? He's promised to come see me, and I need you to help make that happen. There's a free muffin in it for you," she said, winking at me.

In the car on the ride home, I was quiet, because my head was a radio that kept changing stations: the crowd! The music! The clothes! Tío Billy! Then I realized I had forgotten to ask him about something.

"Hey, Tío Billy?" I began. He tilted his chin up and met my eyes in the rearview mirror. "Is—I mean—how—um, how do you . . . when someone's in drag, are they a guy or a girl?" I asked, embarrassed that I had to ask. "Or both?"

"Well, that's kind of a tough question," Tío Billy said, flipping on his turn signal. "A lot of drag queens prefer to be called by their drag names while they're performing or at a gig, so they use 'her' or 'she.' Some don't mind if you call them 'him' or 'he' while they're in drag. Others are transgender women, so they might go by female pronouns all the time."

"Trans women can do drag?" I asked. "Even though they're girls?"

"Sure," Tío Billy said. "Some people even identify as genderfluid, meaning they have different gender identities at different times, or non-binary, which means they don't necessarily identify as male *or* female. Some people use male or female pronouns, some use both, and some use 'they' or 'them.' Anyone can do drag. It doesn't matter what you identify as, but it is important that you be respectful when it comes to correct pronouns," he added.

"But how do you know who goes by what?" I asked. The whole thing sounded very complicated to me, and I was scared I might offend someone by not knowing what to say.

"You just ask," Tío Billy shrugged. That made me nervous. I'm not very good at asking personal questions of people I've only just met. Tío Billy sensed my anxiety. "I think it's always okay to ask, as long as you do it politely. It lets people know that you care about their identity and want to be considerate."

"What do you like to be called?" I wasn't sure if I could get used to calling him Cassie Blanca all the time, but if that's what he preferred, I wanted to try.

"I like to go by RuPaul's rules of engagement," Tío Billy said.

"Who's that?"

"She's the original drag superstar, one of the first drag performers to make a name for herself," he explained. "She said, 'You can call me he, you can call me she, you can call me Regis and Kathie Lee! I don't care, just as long as you call me.'"

I giggled. Whoever this RuPaul is, she's funny.

"I think I'll still call you Tío Billy, if that's okay," I said.

"That's just fine, león," he replied. "And I have to tell you, I'm pretty relieved you liked the show."

"Yeah?" Tío Billy sounded serious, which he almost never is.

"Yeah," he said. "Drag is an important part of who I am, even when I haven't done it in a while. The queer community in this town raised me, in a way, especially after your abuelita died."

"Did Mom ever come to your shows?" I asked.

"She did once or twice, when we were both living here," he said, turning into our neighborhood. "She liked the scene a lot, liked being around all these creative people. But you know her, she's always busy. Painting, teaching, bringing you up all by herself . . ." Tío Billy trailed off, then met my eye. "It means a lot to share this part of my life with you, leoncito."

I didn't know what to say, so I just smiled at Tío

Billy in the mirror. I thought about Mom, and how he must have been sad not to have her at his shows, and then I thought about me. Mom does her best to make it to my Mathletes competitions when she can, but I've never had my dad at . . . well, at anything.

"What's wrong?" Tío Billy asked. I was frowning, deep in thought.

"Did you know my dad?" I asked. "I mean, really know him?"

"Sure," he said, "everybody knew Kevin McLean."

"What do you mean?"

"He was popular. Charming, smart. Cute." Tío Billy gave a wry smile. "Cute enough to get your mom's attention in the middle of her master's thesis, anyway. And he was always running around with that camera. Thought he was gonna be the next Spielberg or something."

"Was he nice?"

"Nice? Nice," he repeated, as though he had never heard the word before. "Yeah, he was nice enough. But it's hard for me to like the guy who left my sister and her kid, you know?"

"Oh," I said, my stomach sinking a little. Clearly, Tío Billy thought Dad was a jerk. I hate to think that's in my genes somewhere, running through my veins, just waiting to manifest and turn me into jerk-spawn.

"Ah, león, I'm sorry," Tío Billy said, reaching back to pat my knee.

"It's okay," I said, "I brought it up. Besides, I like hearing about my dad. I remember some stuff, but I don't actually know that much about him."

"Your mom never talks to you about him?" I shook my head. "Maybe that's for the best. You know, it's tough on her to remember too."

"I know. I don't blame her."

"Well, that's good of you, león. He wasn't a bad guy, your dad. He just wanted different things."

"Different than me?" I asked. Tío Billy's face registered something I couldn't name.

"No," he said firmly as he pulled onto our street. "It has nothing to do with you. Nothing that happened with your mom and dad is your fault, okay? It's no one's fault but his."

I was silent for a minute, just thinking. Talking about the divorce makes me feel like I'm a lost little kid in a grocery store, looking for my mom. It makes me feel sad and scared and like I don't belong anywhere in the world.

But at the show tonight, I was Alice falling down the rabbit hole into Wonderland, where everything was sparkling and wonderful and new. There was a whole world I never knew existed, and it was right under my nose the whole time.

And I belonged there.

I knew it would sound strange to anyone on the outside looking in, but watching that show, I felt more at ease than I ever had before. Sure, I love Mom, and I'm comfortable around Pickle and Carmen, and I'm good at Mathletes. But I felt *alive* being around drag: every inch of me, from my head to my toes, was electrified.

All at once I *knew*. I wanted to do what the drag queens did, to be what they were: bold, confident, full of life. I wanted it all—even if getting it meant putting myself in the spotlight, the place I've always hidden from.

"Tío Billy?" I said, so quietly it was barely a whisper. "Can seventh graders do All-Ages Night?"

He parked the car in the driveway and turned around to face me.

"Are you serious, león?"

I nodded solemnly. "I loved it," I said. "I really loved it."

Tío Billy blinked, looking so surprised I thought he might fall over. Then he started smiling, wider and wider.

"Of course. Of course they can," he said, "I told you: anyone can do drag."

☆ 5 ☆

I could barely sleep at all that night. I stared at my glow-in-the-dark stars and wondered what it would be like to have that kind of confidence, that kind of poise. The thought of getting up on stage before a room full of people and performing made my stomach flip-flop, but in a good way. It was anticipation, not fear. Well, maybe a little fear. But who needed to know?

I was still awake when the birds started chirping, but I didn't feel tired. I got out of bed as soon as I heard Tío Billy stirring downstairs.

"Hey, león," he said when I appeared in the kitchen. He was scrambling eggs at the stove, the air rich with the smell of butter melting in the pan. "You're up awfully early for a Sunday."

"I've got a tournament today," I said, heading to the fridge for orange juice. "Mathletes."

"Ah," he crooned, swirling the eggs around with his spatula. "Home or away?"

"It's at Eastern Greene," I said. "So only like twenty minutes from here."

"They any good?"

I giggled and shook my head. Tío Billy hooted in amusement.

"Ha! 'Atta boy," he said. "You want some breakfast?"

Tío Billy and I ate our eggs and toast together in relative silence, enjoying the shiny newness of the morning. But everything reminded me of drag: The glint of light off my fork was like a disco ball, a sprinkle of salt was glitter raining down onto the crowd. I was obsessed. *How long am I supposed to wait before I bring this up again to Tío Billy? Is there drag etiquette? Protocol? Do I have to wait to be spirited away in the dead of the night by a bunch of drag queens before I can become one myself, or something? What would you call a group of drag queens anyway? A sparkle? A monarchy? A glamour?*

"So," Tío Billy said, interrupting my racing thoughts. "Have you given any more thought to what you said last night?" A little thrill went through me.

"You mean All-Ages Night," I said. "Yeah, I have."

"And?"

"And I still want to do it," I said. "I thought about it all night."

A smile danced across Tío Billy's face, but then something in his expression changed. He put his fork down and cleared his throat.

"You know, león," he began, "doing drag is a wonderful thing. It changed my life and gave me a whole other family. A weird, kooky, colorful family," he laughed, "but a family all the same. But I want you to go into this with your eyes wide open."

"What do you mean?"

"I mean there are people in this life who are going to try to put down anybody they perceive as different. And sometimes drag queens, and also the queer community in general, can fall into that category," he said. "Now, there's nothing wrong with being queer or doing drag. There's something wrong with the people who think otherwise, if you ask me! But you might get nasty comments anyway for being a drag queen. You might get teased. You might find out that some of the people around you aren't as accepting as you once believed. Do you know what I mean?"

I did, and I knew he was right. Middle schoolers could be especially vicious—just look at Nelson. And yes, I dreaded my classmates finding out I loved drag, but that was nothing compared to how badly I wanted to try it.

"I know," I said. "But I want to anyway. I just . . . want to see if I can."

"Well, I *know* you can," Tío Billy said. "That goes without saying."

"And if I won," I reasoned, "a thousand dollars could buy me a really great telescope. Like a professional grade one!"

"That's true," chuckled. "With that kind of money you could buy yourself a whole fleet of telescopes."

"So will you help me?" I asked, turning to him. "Will you help me learn drag?"

"You don't even have to ask, león," he said. I grinned. "First things first, you're going to need a drag name."

I hadn't even thought about that. I've been Martin McLean my whole life. It was hard to imagine being anybody else.

"I'm not very good at coming up with names," I admitted. "I think I've named every character in my creative writing assignments 'Martin.'"

"You could just stay Martin," he reasoned, taking a sip of juice. "Queens have definitely done that before. But most choose something different, something that they feel represents their inner, more fabulous self. Sometimes it's a funny name, sometimes it's very dramatic and glamorous."

"Jeez," I said, "how does anyone choose?"

"I think the most important thing is that you pick a name that means something to you, right down in your bones," he said, chewing. "You know what I mean, león?"

I felt a spark ignite in my heart, a rush of realization.

"What about that?" I asked. "León."

"Ooh," Tío Billy said, catching on. "Yes! I like it. I think you'd need a first name, though. It has to roll off the tongue. Maybe something with a little alliteration?"

"Okay," I said. "Like what?"

"Liza?" he tried. I shook my head—it wasn't quite right. "Lola?"

"No, but that's close." I drummed my fingers against the table, wracking my brain. Then: "I've got it!" I cried. "Lottie. Lottie León."

It was perfect. I liked the way it tripped about in my mouth, the long *la* cut off gracefully by the *ti*, the roundness of the *ón*.

A thrill ran through me when I said the name. There it was: my drag alter ego. Lottie León was someone who could conquer the world. She wasn't afraid of the sound of her own voice—she wasn't afraid of *anything*. I didn't know her very well yet, but I did know one thing: I wanted to follow in Lottie León's fabulous footsteps.

"Lottie León," Tío Billy said, trying it on for size with a cheeky smile. "I love it. I think you've got your name, Miss León!" He stood up from the table to clear his plate. "Now you just need an act."

An act! The most important part and the part I was most afraid of. I had no idea how to perform in front of an audience. How in the world could I learn to do it in just a few months?

"Hey, león?" Tío Billy said. He cocked his head toward the clock above the stove. "You keeping an eye on the time?"

Shoot! Figuring out a drag queen training program would have to wait. It was time to get ready for Mathletes. I thanked Tío Billy for breakfast and ran back upstairs to get dressed. My Mathletes uniform is awful: khaki pants, a gray pullover sweater with a blue button-down beneath it, finished off with a terrible plaid tie. All tucked in neatly and nerdily. I guess it could be worse; the girls look like extras on *Little House on the Prairie* in their lumpy blue sweaters and plaid skirts that go down to their calves. The Mathletes community isn't exactly a hotbed of fashion.

Around 7, Mom roused herself and started her coffee. She doesn't really become a person until 8, but on competition days she does her best to join the land of the living. By 7:30 we were in the car, Mom in her bathrobe and bonnet and me in my itchy sweater. Technically, we were supposed to be dropped off at school by 7:15 so Mr. Peterson could drive us as a group to tournaments on the Mathletes bus. But Mom was *always* running late, so rather than hold everyone else up, she usually drove me straight to the competition herself.

"So," she began in between yawns, "what'd you think of Miss Cassie Blanca?"

I blinked and whirled my head toward her in surprise.

"You knew he was taking me to a drag show?" I yelped.

Mom gave me a dubious look. "You think I would let my little brother take my baby boy out somewhere without knowing where? Please." She reached over and tapped my arm playfully with her fist. "So? Did you have fun?"

"It was . . . the greatest," I said.

"I had a feeling you would like it," Mom said. "You know, when Billy first started doing drag, I thought it was so strange. I knew he was gay, and I knew other queer people, too, but I had never seen anything like drag. It was so . . . flashy. I didn't understand why he had to be so, yo no sé, so *public* about it all. Couldn't he have a different hobby? Something that called a little less attention to himself?" She shook her head, as if she couldn't believe her past self. "I was afraid for him, afraid that people wouldn't accept him. And then, I went to one of his shows."

"What did you think?" *Wait, does Mom even*

approve of drag? Tío Billy said she did, but . . .
Suddenly, my chest was tight, but Mom smiled.

"I thought it was incredible," she said, her eyes sparkling. "I saw my brother up there, looking happier than he had in a long, long time, and I realized that drag was just another form of expression, like my painting. It's his art."

"It's beautiful!" I gushed. "I can't believe I didn't know we had drag in Bloomington!"

"Oh, sure. Your Tío Billy actually helped the scene take off here. You know, you remind me so much of him, when he was a kid," Mom said.

"Really?"

"Oh, yeah. You're both smart and sensitive, with a good head on your shoulders. You even look a little like him," she said. "You're a lot alike. That's one of the reasons I thought it would be good for him to stay with us for a while."

My stomach went sour at the thought of how I'd flipped out on Mom the night Tío Billy arrived. I bit my lip, trying to find the right words.

"Mom?" I said. "I'm really sorry for yelling at you the other night."

"Oh yeah?" she said lightly, not meeting my eye.

"Yeah. It was . . ."

"Uncalled for?" she suggested. I nodded.

"I thought maybe you had called Tío Billy because . . . because you thought I was like him in *other* ways too. And maybe you thought that if it was true, it would be . . . bad." I heard Mom suck in a sharp burst of air, and I knew she understood what I was trying to say.

"Mijo," she said, "I love my brother for exactly who he is, and I love you for exactly who *you* are. And I will support you no matter what." She looked over to me and squeezed my hand. "It really did just work out that Billy was going to be headed this way anyway. But I do think he'll be a good person for you to have in your life—even if he's bound to get on my nerves a little while he's here!" she said, rolling her eyes. I smiled and squeezed her hand back. *What a relief.*

She dropped me off at Eastern Greene Middle School with a big wet kiss on the head and a wave, which in Mom language means "Love you, pick you up at 6." I waved back as she drove off. Inside, I checked the room assignment sheet posted in the lunchroom, then went in search of my team. The pre-tournament ruckus was already in full swing when I opened the door to the homeroom.

"Give it back!" Poppy was crying, grasping at her sketchbook, which was held aloft by Nelson.

"Aww, *give it back!*" he mocked, dangling it just out of reach.

"Enough, Nelson!" Mariam called from where she was perched on top of a desk, applying her lip gloss. "You're not funny. Like, at all."

"It's not a comedy routine," J.P. said, looking up from the caricatures of the team he was drawing (badly) on the chalkboard. "It's a mating ritual."

"Hey!" Nelson scowled, lowering his guard just long enough for Poppy to leap up and grab her sketchbook.

"Ha!" she laughed triumphantly, hugging the sketchbook protectively to her chest. She shot a dirty look at Nelson and retreated to her corner of the room, next to Mariam.

"We should really be practicing," Konrad said, wringing his hands.

"We're going to be fine," Chris said, guiding Konrad back to a seated position. "Hey, Martin!" I raised my hand in an awkward wave. "Good timing. Things were just starting to come off the rails over here." He shot an accusing look at Nelson, who was pouting and repeatedly returning his gaze to Poppy. "Mr. Peterson stepped out for a second," he explained, "so I guess that means you have the bridge!"

He chuckled at his own joke, then blinked at me. "You know, the bridge? Like on a ship? Because you're the captain?"

"Oh!" I said, finally realizing what he meant. "Oh, right."

"Sorry," he said, suddenly bashful. "It was a bad joke." Chris blushed, his tanned face glowing from within like a summer sunrise.

"No, no, it was good!" I said. "I'm just a little slow this morning. A lot on my mind."

"You're not worried, are you?" he asked. "Because the Eastern Greene kids are a total joke. I heard one of them is a ninth grader they held back specifically so they could have a chance this year," he whispered, leaning in close. "But that's just a rumor."

"That'd be wild," I said, and he nodded, eyes wide. I realized we were standing super close, and my face got hot. I jumped back. "But, no, I've just been really busy lately. It's nothing."

"Okay!" Mr. Peterson glided into the room, resplendent in his pleated khakis and forest green argyle sweater. "Here are the schedules for the day, hot off the press." He placed a stack of paper on one of the front desks. We all scrambled to grab a copy, eager to see who was competing when, and in what events. Everyone competes in the individual rounds, but the team rounds and countdown rounds require groups of four and three, respectively. Mr. Peterson knows who does best in what rounds, but he prefers to mix us up. He says it helps us train and grow as students and competitors, which is all fine and good—but I still want to win.

"Looks like it's you, me, Nelson, and Poppy for team," Chris said. I scowled. Chris and I work pretty well together and Poppy is brilliant (if a little scatterbrained), but it's impossible to work with

Nelson in any time-efficient manner, and we only get twenty minutes to solve ten very difficult questions.

"Aw, cute," Nelson sneered from behind us, "it'll be like a double date."

My stomach dropped to my toenails. I had hoped that Nelson would have dropped this string of insults by now. I opened my mouth to speak, but Poppy beat me to it.

"As if I'd ever date pond scum like you," she said, rolling her eyes at Nelson. "Ignore him," she said to me. "We're going to kick a . . . I mean, butt." Mr. Peterson cast her a warning look, and she caught herself from swearing with a rueful smirk.

"I also have some good news," Mr. Peterson said, once everyone had perused the schedule. "The date for Regionals has been set."

"Ooh!" Mariam clapped her hands together with a grin.

"I'm glad you're excited, but we have to qualify first," Mr. Peterson said with a smile. "*If* we end up qualifying, the big day will be Saturday, January 27th, 7 p.m."

Immediately there was a rushing in my ears, and my whole body went cold. *There must be some mistake. It can't be the 27th. It* can't.

"W-wait," I stammered, "are you sure? January 27th?"

"Yes," Mr. Peterson answered, perplexed. "Is there a problem?"

"What? No. No, sorry, no," I said, shaking my head. Mr. Peterson shrugged and went back to making notes on his copy of the schedule. I sank into a nearby desk. *This isn't happening. What about All-Ages Night?* I was so wrapped up in thought, I barely noticed when Chris sat down next to me, his brows knit in worry.

"Are you okay?" he asked. "You got super pale."

"I'm fine," I said. "Just like, whoa, Regionals, right?"

"Totally," he agreed. "And it'd be your first one as team captain! That's kind of major."

"Major," I repeated. "Sorry, I guess I'm not fully awake yet."

It was a bad excuse, but it was the best I could do. My mind was reeling. What are the chances that the two most important nights of my whole entire life so far would end up being the *same* night? And how could I possibly do both if we *did* end up qualifying for Regionals?

"Well, you better snap out of it!" Chris said, good-naturedly clapping me on the shoulder. "We can't win without you, Martin."

We can't win without you, Martin. His voice echoed in my head, as he walked away. There's no way I could bail on my team—not for Regionals, and definitely not my first Regionals as captain. But unless someone invented a time machine, I didn't know how I would make it work.

I was distracted for the entire day. I managed to compete, and I think I did okay, but it was like my body had shown up to the tournament without me. Whatever brain power I didn't need to solve the math problems posed to our team, I was using to work on a much different problem: *How could I do two competitions in one night?*

I definitely didn't solve that problem at the podium.

We ended up winning silver medals, but I didn't feel like I had earned mine. Mr. Peterson, apparently, disagreed.

"Well done today, Martin," he said as we headed out of the school. "I was worried about you in that timed target round, but you bounced back. And you and Chris seemed to make a good team; I might have to pair you up more often."

"Yeah," I said, not really listening. "Thanks."

When I got out to the parking lot, it was Tío Billy waiting for me, not Mom. I made a quizzical face at him through the window before getting in the backseat.

"Hey, león!" he said with a big grin. "How'd you do?"

"Good," I said. "Second place."

"Congrats, man! That's nothing to sneeze at. Hey, I got you something."

"You did?" I asked. "It's not my birthday."

"I know that," he laughed. "This is a 'just because'

gift, all right? Check the passenger seat."

I reached over the center console and into the seat next to Tío Billy, where there was a department store shopping bag waiting for me. I pulled it into the back and dug into it, throwing tissue paper aside to uncover a glossy white shoebox.

"Shoes?" I asked. Tío Billy waved at me.

"Just open it!"

I pried the lid off the shoebox and peeked inside. A flash of silver caught my eye, and I pulled aside more tissue to reveal a pair of sparkling pumps, covered entirely in glitter. My jaw dropped. They shone like a star I could hold in my hands.

"Wow," was all I could say. I turned the shoes over, admiring their graceful arch and slope and their towering heels.

"They're your size," Tío Billy said, and I realized he had been watching me. "I picked them out today. What do you think?"

"They're . . . beautiful," I said. "They look just like the ones Aida Lott wore!"

"I thought you might like them," he said, beaming. "Every drag queen needs a great pair of heels. Consider this the first building block in creating Lottie León."

I closed my eyes and imagined myself wearing the shoes, shining like moonstones on my feet. One of the many things my favorite performer in the whole world, Celia Cruz, was famous for was her shoes. Now I could be just like her! (Okay, not *just* like her—Celia's shoes were beautiful works of art that she eventually had to get custom-made especially for her. Mine came from a department store. But a boy could dream!) I imagined myself walking around the way the queens did, as though I owned the stage and the entire world too.

And then I imagined myself falling flat on my face, toppling from the tall heights of my heels like a satellite from the upper atmosphere.

"I don't know if I can walk in these," I said, suddenly anxious. I hurriedly started to put the shoes back in their box, but Tío Billy reached back and stilled my hands, already slick with sweat.

"Hey," he said gently, "don't worry. That's what I'm here for. We'll have you slaying the runway in no time."

I felt my phone vibrate inside my pocket, so I shifted the shoes and box on my lap and fished it out to find a bunch of notifications:

★ ★ ★

ReadMe App
SEPT. 17—6:24 P.M.

PicknLittle: Martin, my boy!
LadyOfTheStage: Maaaaaartin, are you done at Mathletes yet?

PicknLittle: Mrs. Randolph rather rudely assigned homework over the weekend.

LadyOfTheStage: Who does that in the first week of school?

PicknLittle: It's almost the third week, Carmen.

LadyOfTheStage: I said what I said.

PicknLittle: Anyway, chemistry is way too close to math for my liking, so I need to know what your answer was for #7.

LadyOfTheStage: Martin, don't let him pressure you

LadyOfTheStage: But also I need your answer for #13

LadyOfTheStage: In exchange, I promise to help you with the Shakespeare we have to read for English.

PicknLittle: Bribery? Shakes*please.*

mathletesmartin: Sorry, guys, I can't talk right now—I'm in the car with my uncle.

mathletesmartin: Maybe later?

PicknLittle: Boo

PicknLittle: Booooooooo.

LadyOfTheStage: Ugh, fiiiiiiine. But don't forget about us!

Carmen and Pickle's homework could wait, especially when I had a much bigger problem: two competitions, one night, and zero ideas on how to make it all happen. I carefully tucked the heels away in their glitter-speckled paper, closed the box, and hugged it tight against myself.

"They're perfect," I said. "Thank you, Tío Billy."

"De nada," he said, starting up the car.

"I sort of have some bad news, though." I didn't want to tell him, because telling him would make the whole mess real. But he had to know—so he could help me figure out what to do. "I don't know if we're competing yet, but . . . Regionals is the same day as All-Ages Night."

"Seriously?" I nodded. Tío Billy groaned, sucking air through his teeth. "Ay, tremendo paquete. Shoot. That's no good. How do you want to play this?"

"I don't know how I could do both," I admitted, "but if I could . . ." He smiled a little in the rearview mirror.

"We've got some time, right? When will you find out if you qualify?"

"Late October or early November, probably," I said.

"And it's only September," he said. "We'll figure it out."

He pulled out of the parking lot and onto the street, the Spanish pop station playing softly in the background. I rested my head against the window and watched the street lights blink past, dancing in my eyes like disco lights.

I knew it was possible that I could try drag and fail at it miserably. I knew it was possible that I could try it and hate it and never, ever want to look at a pair of heels again.

But there was a part of me—a part that grew every second—that really believed I could be good at being Lottie León. I might even be great. Wouldn't it be worth it to try, just to know if I could?

Mathletes might be my past and present, I thought, *but Lottie León is part of my future.*

OCTOBER

ReadMe App
OCT. 22—3:01 PM

mathletesmartin: Hey!

PicknLittle: Dude, where have you been?

LadyOfTheStage: Hi, breaking in new T-straps is the worst and I long for death. What's new?

mathletesmartin: Pickle is yelling at me.

LadyOfTheStage: ...I asked what's *new*.

PicknLittle: You have been a complete spaceman for the past couple weeks.

mathletesmartin: What does that even mean?

PicknLittle: Spacy

PicknLittle: Floaty

PicknLittle: Extremely difficult to reach without the help of rocket boosters and incredibly long-distance phone service!

mathletesmartin: Is it possible, dearest Pickle, that you are being a tad dramatic?

LadyOfTheStage: Ooh, intrigue. You usually reserve the D word for me.

PicknLittle: I'm not being dramatic, I'm telling it like it is!

LadyOfTheStage: You have been a little weird lately

mathletesmartin: Weird how?!

LadyOfTheStage: I don't know. You don't say much in class.

mathletesmartin: I'm learning!

LadyOfTheStage: Or at lunch

mathletesmartin: I'm eating!

LadyOfTheStage: Or on the bus

mathletesmartin: I'm...

LadyOfTheStage: Don't say commuting, that's just sad.

PicknLittle: Plus, you haven't said a single thing about me and Violet.

mathletesmartin: What about you and Violet?

PicknLittle: ??!???

LadyOfTheStage: Oh, Martin...

PicknLittle: We're totally a thing!

mathletesmartin: Since when?!

LadyOfTheStage: Since Pickle took her to Bloomington Days last week.

mathletesmartin: Bloomington Days was last week?

PicknLittle: See!

mathletesmartin: Pickle got a girlfriend and I didn't even notice?

mathletesmartin: Jeez. I'm really sorry.

LadyOfTheStage: Well…not exactly…

PicknLittle: She's not my girlfriend, per se.

mathletesmartin: Oooookay… ?

PicknLittle: We held hands.

LadyOfTheStage: And tell him about the bracelet!

PicknLittle: It's a cuff, Carmen. Men wear cuffs.

LadyOfTheStage: Violet made him a bracelet. A looooove bracelet.

PicknLittle: It is a CUFF and it's cool.

mathletesmartin: Is it purple?

LadyOfTheStage: It's purple.

PicknLittle: It is nONE OF YOUR BUSINESS since apparently you don't even care enough to notice that we're totally pre-dating.

mathletesmartin: I didn't know pre-dating was a thing

LadyOfTheStage: (Me neither)

mathletesmartin: (Why are we typing like this?)

LadyOfTheStage: (We're whispering)

mathletesmartin: (Oh! Cool.)

PicknLittle: I CAN SEE YOU, INGRATES

mathletesmartin: Pickle, I really am sorry. I've just been super busy with captain stuff for Mathletes practices.

PicknLittle: You don't have practice on weekends, though.

mathletesmartin: Unless there's a tournament

PicknLittle: Your next one isn't for another two weeks.

mathletesmartin: So?

LadyOfTheStage: So what Pickle's trying to say is that we miss you. You've been spending a lot of time with your team lately

LadyOfTheStage: And I get that! Because you're the captain now and that's mega-awesome and important.

PicknLittle: Buuut then we never see you when you're not with them either.

LadyOfTheStage: Right

mathletesmartin: You guys, you know my uncle is in town. I've never really gotten to hang out with him this much.

PicknLittle: He's been in town for like, almost two months, dude.

mathletesmartin: I know.

LadyOfTheStage: We're not trying to gang up on you! We'd just like for our prodigal friend to return. We miss you. Right, Pickle?

PicknLittle: Well …

LadyOfTheStage: Pickle.

PicknLittle: Yeah, yeah, okay

PicknLittle: Even though it totally ruins my street cred to say so, yeah, I guess we kind of miss you.

LadyOfTheStage: Heh. Street cred. As if.

PicknLittle: Hey! I have cred! I have tons of cred!

PicknLittle: I have cred coming out the wazoo! Out the ying-yang!

LadyOfTheStage: Says the man wearing the purple bracelet.

PicknLittle: IT'S A CUFF

mathletesmartin: Hey, guys, I gotta go. Can we meet at B-Town tonight? Milkshakes on me.

PicknLittle: Milkshakes, you say?

LadyOfTheStage: Ooh, I'm in

mathletesmartin: 7ish?

PicknLittle: I'll bring my bracelet.

LadyOfTheStage: Hah!

☆ 6 ☆

You wouldn't *believe* how badly my feet hurt.

Tío Billy and I were spending every afternoon (except for the ones I had Mathletes) working on a routine for Lottie León. Sometimes we'd go to Hoosier Mama and practice in the basement, with Dorie dropping in periodically to feed us her latest cookie creations, but most of the time I was in the living room at home, learning how to be Lottie.

And it was *hard*. There's so much energy involved, learning to stand up straight and remembering to keep your shoulders back. And girls walk so differently from boys! There was more of a sway to the way Lottie walked. I wasn't used to carrying myself like her—like someone with confidence. At first, Tío Billy was teaching me to walk como una princesa in my bare feet because it's easier. But soon it was time to start practicing in my beautiful sparkly heels.

"Okay, upsy-daisy," Tío Billy said, standing and holding out his hands to me. The silver pumps made my feet look delicate even though I felt anything but. He pulled me to my feet and I immediately started teetering, my arms pinwheeling at my sides. Tío Billy leapt forward, steadying me. When I was upright, I realized my legs were suddenly much longer—or at least, they felt that way. I would have to extend my leg *much* farther if I was going to would make a step happen. "All right, león, let's see baby's first steps! Aw, I feel like I should be videotaping," Tío Billy teased.

"Very funny," I muttered, too focused on my task to muster up a better response. I stared down at my feet and tried to inch one foot forward just one step. The heels made a satisfying *CLACK* on the hardwood floors. I took another step, then another. "Hey, this isn't so hard!" I exclaimed, enjoying the purposeful feeling behind each noisy step. I turned in a small circle and caught a glimpse of myself in the hall mirror. I looked completely ridiculous in my Iron Man T-shirt and track pants pulled up to my knees, but I had to admit, the shoes didn't look half bad. I put a hand on my hip, watching myself in the mirror just to see how it would feel. I looked completely silly, like a lamp pole with an attitude.

"You gotta loosen up, león," Tío Billy said, coming up behind me. He took my shoulders in his hands and gently shook my arms back and forth until they were hanging limp at my sides. "Relax your arms and legs."

"I'll fall over!"

"No, you won't," Tío Billy laughed. "I promise. It's all about confidence, right? And the trick to confidence is to fake it till you make it."

"Just pretend?" I asked. It was hard for me to imagine Tío Billy ever having to pretend to be confident.

"Sure," he replied, "everyone does it." He indicated with his hand that I should lift my chin. "There you go. And straighten out your back." I did, trying to draw myself up to the tallest I could be. "Good! Now pop your hip a little."

"Pop?"

"Yeah, like this." He demonstrated by jutting out his hip to one side. "Put all your weight on one leg, and let the other side sort of relax. The hip bearing your weight should be higher than the other. Does that make sense?"

I tried it, suddenly shifting all my weight into my right leg. Immediately I lost my balance, the heel slipping out from under me and sending me to the floor in a skittering heap. I landed funny on my tailbone, and the blunt pain radiated up my throat into a lump of embarrassment.

"Ouch," I mumbled, keeping my head down to disguise the tears that were forming. I hated being such a llorón, a crybaby, but the frustration was overwhelming me. Maybe I could walk up and down a stage, but when it came to doing the hard stuff—like heels and dancing and confidence—I was a complete failure.

"Hey, it's okay," Tío Billy said, helping me back up. He saw the wince of pain on my face and hugged me. "It's hard for everybody the first time."

"If I can't walk in these shoes, everyone's going to think I'm a loser," I said softly. The bruise from the fall was forming beneath my skin like a dull roar. "Just one more thing for them to laugh at."

"First of all, don't worry about the shoes. They take time to get used to. And second of all, who cares what other people think?" He gently tilted my chin so that I had to look at him. "I mean it: who cares?"

"I care!" I said, exploding into tears. "I care what they think! Because it's bad enough everyone thinks I'm quiet and weird, now when people find out I'm a drag queen, I won't even be a good one!"

I kicked off the shoes and threw myself onto the couch, staring up at the ceiling Mom had painted in robin's egg blue. I was acting like a toddler, but I didn't care. My feelings were a big boiling pot inside my chest, and soon they were going to spill out all over everyone. Tío Billy came over and moved my legs so he could sit next to me.

"León," he said, "let me ask you something."

"Okay," I sniffled into my sleeve.

"What's so wrong with being a drag queen?"

His question took me by surprise. I sat up to face him.

"N-nothing," I stammered, "I didn't mean—I just—I didn't mean to offend you or anything."

"Oh, I'm not offended." Tío Billy waved the notion away with his hand. "I'm asking you. You seem to think if your classmates find out that you want to be a drag queen, they'll make fun of you. Why would they do that?"

"Because . . ." I thought for a moment. "Because that's just not something boys do."

"I'm a boy," Tío Billy said, "and I do drag. Drag was started specifically *for* boys."

"Well, right," I said, "but it's not something normal boys do."

"Normal, huh? What is normal, anyway?" he asked with a smile. "Who decides what's normal?"

I knew what wasn't normal at my school, and I knew why everyone would make fun of me, but I didn't want to say it to Tío Billy. He nudged me gently with his elbow and caught my eye. "What is it, león?"

"It's just that . . . people will think I'm gay," I said very quietly. Tío Billy made a small noise and looked at me intently.

"And what's the problem with being gay?" he

asked. It wasn't mean or accusing—just a question. "When you love someone, that's a wonderful thing, right? So who cares *who* you love? What matters is that you *do* love."

I took a deep breath. I was sure I had fallen in love with drag, but when I thought of what it would mean to love someone else . . . well, I didn't feel sure of anything. Tío Billy was always so confident in who he was, but what if he expected that of me, right away?

"I don't know what I am," I admitted, staring at my aching toes. "Is that okay?"

"Of course it is! León, you're so young. I know it doesn't feel like it right now, but I swear to you: you don't have to have everything figured out," he said. "At twelve years old, I didn't know anything about anything. I just knew I liked how I looked with lipstick on, and that sometimes it was fun to put on silly outfits and dance around." I giggled, mostly out of sheer relief. It was hard for me to imagine there ever being a time when Tío Billy didn't know exactly who he was, but it made me feel better to know that there had been. After all, he turned out okay. There could be hope for me too.

Tío Billy put his arm around me. "There's a lot of pressure in this world to be a certain way, to meet certain standards," he said. "But you don't have to give in to that pressure, even if it's coming from within you."

"Within me?"

"Sure. Sometimes, you can know who you are and what you want in your heart, but try and smother it because you know it's different from what the world wants you to be," he said. "But nobody knows you better than you do. Yours is the only voice you need to listen to."

"My voice is kind of quiet," I said.

"That's okay too. You don't have to be the loudest león on the plains to be the king. You just have to be the one willing to fight for what you want. Get those claws out, you know?" he winked.

"I want to try to be Lottie," I said, "I have to."

"Good," Tío Billy said. He stood up and stuck out his hand to me. "Then let's keep trying."

★ ★ ★

I locked up my bike outside B-Town Diner with my feet swelling inside my Adidas. By the time we had finished practicing, I could walk in a straight line almost perfectly, and I could turn in a circle. Walking backward had been a challenge (I almost pulled down Mom's drapes a few times), but Tío Billy assured me it wasn't a skill I'd have to use too often if I didn't want to. I was excited to be making progress, until I pried off the heels and saw my blisters. Yuck.

Pickle and Carmen were already at our favorite

booth, the one all the way in the back. Pickle likes it because he says it makes him feel mysterious, like a mob boss waiting for someone to walk in and kiss his ring. Carmen likes it because it's nearest to the kitchen (she loves her loaded fries piping hot) and because it's perfectly situated for eavesdropping on everyone else in the place. I just like it because it's farthest from everyone else and there's never a draft.

Pickle was hanging out of the booth, waving his arm. I shuffled past a group of college kids pouring out of their table and made my way to the booth, resplendent in its gray vinyl upholstery. Pickle was wearing his favorite pea coat and a stocking cap; Carmen had donned a denim jacket over a mustard yellow blouse and bedazzled jeans.

"Took the liberty of ordering you your usual," she said, sliding a strawberry milkshake toward me as I settled in on Pickle's side of the booth. She was fiddling with the straw on her cake batter milkshake and looking to Pickle.

"You're late," he said, He was already nearly halfway through his chocolate shake.

"I know, I'm sorry," I said. "But I'm really glad to see you guys."

"Us too!" Carmen chirped. "I've spent so much time in the performing arts center, it was starting to feel like the whole universe was a set of concrete walls and a stage."

"How's the musical coming along?" I asked.

"Oh, fine," she said. "At least, it will be. Turns out Didi is allergic to the chocolate Lip Smackers that Turner put on before their big kiss scene. She'll be all right, once the swelling goes down." Carmen smiled wickedly and took a big swig of her milkshake. Didi Esposito got the lead role over Carmen and has since become her archnemesis.

"Too bad," Pickle said, taking a gravy-covered fry from the plate in the middle of the slightly sticky table. A flash of purple peeked out from under his sleeve. "Maybe if it had been worse, you could have stepped in."

"Now, now, let's not wish bad things unto others," Carmen said grandly, feigning a haughty air. "Besides, there's no one else who could play Madame de la Grande Bouche as well as me."

"Doesn't that mean 'Mrs. Big Mouth'?" I asked. Pickle choked on his milkshake. Carmen frowned.

"It *does,* thank you very much!"

"What a coincidence," Pickle said, his voice high and tight with laughter.

"You guys are the worst!" Carmen pouted.

"You loooove us," Pickle crooned.

"We've not even been here fifteen minutes and you're already picking on me," Carmen said. "Unbelievable."

"Oh, you totally believe it," I said, dragging a cheesy fry through some gravy before popping it in my mouth. I had forgotten just how good it felt to hang with Pickle and Carmen, listening to them bicker, basking in the happy glow of friends.

"Okay, enough! Our first order of business: Halloween." Carmen clapped her hands together excitedly.

"What about it?" I said around a mouthful of fry.

"It's next week, duh," Carmen said. "What are we going to be?"

"Aw, Carmen, not this again," Pickle moaned, putting his head in his hands. Every year, Carmen tried to convince us all to do a group costume, and every year, Pickle and I put up a big fight. But we always ended up giving in to Carmen's whims. Last year we went as the Three Musketeers, with twirly fake mustaches and everything. Our best was in fourth grade, when we went as a BLT—me as bacon, Carmen as tomato, and Pickle as lettuce. It took three weeks for the green dye to completely wash out of his hair.

"Come on, we have to keep the streak alive!" Carmen begged. "Any ideas?"

"Yes, you two go as whatever you want, and I'll go as a corpse, because over my dead body will I let Violet see me in some silly getup," Pickle said.

"Ooh, I didn't even think about Violet," Carmen mused. "Do you think she'd want to join us? Having a fourth would open up a whole new world of possibilities."

"Right, because asking my sort-of-not-really-girlfriend to do some wacky group costume with us is *definitely* not going to scare her off or anything," Pickle said.

"Pickle!" Carmen pleaded, putting on her puppy dog eyes.

"No."

"Pickle."

"No!"

"*Pickle!*"

"Fine!" Pickle threw his hands up in the air, exasperated. "I'll ask her! But when she says no, calls us all freaks, and leaves me, it'll be your fault!"

"I can live with that," Carmen replied primly. "Okay, ideas? Assuming we're a foursome, that is."

"We could be the Scooby-Doo gang?" I offered. "I bet Pickle and Violet would make a great Fred and Daphne."

"Yeah, but then we'd need a dog, and my little Woofecito isn't exactly the Scooby type," Carmen said, shaking her head. "Have you ever seen a bichon solve a crime?"

"Let's be Pac Man and the ghosts. That way I can cover my face in shame," Pickle moaned. Carmen and I both rolled our eyes.

"Ooh, what about Peter Pan?" Carmen exclaimed, her eyes bright. "I've always wanted to go as Captain Hook. The mustache, the hat, the hook! I love it!"

"That's not bad," Pickle mused begrudgingly. "Violet and I could be Peter and Wendy."

"Aww!" Carmen squealed. "That is so cute! So Martin, that leaves Tinkerbell for you!"

"What? But Tinkerbell is a girl!" I said, my stomach dropping. There was no way I could go to school as Tinkerbell. What if people saw me and knew, just *knew* somehow about me and drag? What if something about me gave it away? Tío Billy's voice rang out in my head—*What's so wrong with being a drag queen? Who decides what's normal?*—but the panic was creeping up, threatening to overwhelm me.

"So?" Carmen said, waving her hand. "It'll be fun! You can have a blonde wig and wings. I bet those beat up old tennis shoes would even look okay with some white leggings," Carmen said, gently kicking my sore feet under the table. "C'mon, it'll be so funny!"

"It's not funny!" I snapped. Carmen blinked in surprise.

"Fine, jeez," she said, obviously bristling. "I guess you can be Mr. Smee, or whatever."

Instantly, I felt bad for yelling at Carmen. But the idea of going to school as a girl made my palms clammy and my stomach ache.

The world's longest minute passed in silence. Carmen stared at the other tables, I stared at my milkshake, and Pickle stared at both of us uncomfortably.

"Sooo," Pickle warbled, breaking the silence and turning to me. "What have you been up to lately?"

"I told you, I've been doing Mathletes stuff and hanging with Tío Billy."

"Right, but like . . ."

"Pickle's trying to ask why you wouldn't rather be with us," Carmen said, matter-of-fact.

"Exactly," Pickle said, placing his hands on the table seriously. "What's the deal?"

"Deal? There's no deal," I said, stammering. "I don't know. We just hang out."

"Didi said she saw you and your uncle at Hoosier Mama the other night talking to some butch lady," Carmen said, twirling her straw without meeting my eye.

"Well, Didi is a big gossip."

"That's true," she said. "But I don't know, it's not like we really care what you do."

"Then why ask?" I grumbled. "Why are you even talking to Didi anyway? I thought you hated her."

"I do," replied Carmen airily. "But we have to spend a lot of time together in rehearsal, and when she said she saw you there, I thought it was weird."

"What's weird about it? It's just a coffee shop."

"Okay, first of all, you hate coffee," Carmen said, ticking off the number one on her fingers. "And second of all . . . well . . ." She looked at Pickle, seemingly for support. He sighed.

"Dude, Didi has kind of been spreading around this . . . not a rumor, but . . . she's been telling everybody that Hoosier Mama kind of has a reputation," he said.

"What do you mean, a reputation?"

"It's not bad, it's just . . ." Carmen trailed off again.

"I guess the night crowd there is a little different," Pickle said. "Didi said it's sort of known around town as a place where certain people hang out."

"Certain people?" I repeated.

"Gay people," Carmen said, obviously trying very hard to be nonchalant. "It's kind of a place where lots of gay people hang out, I guess—I don't know, that's just what Didi said—and so after she saw you there with your uncle, she wanted to know if your uncle was gay."

"You know he is," I said defensively. "What's the big deal?"

"There isn't one," Carmen said quickly. "It's just that after Didi asked about your uncle—and I told her it was none of her business and she should keep her big mouth shut, by the way—she wanted to know . . ."

"Know what?" But I knew what was coming.

". . . if *you* were gay," Carmen finished.

"What? No! I mean, I don't know." My tongue was like lead in my mouth. "What the hell, Carmen?"

"Don't shoot the messenger!" she cried. "I just thought you'd want to know what people were saying."

"People? What people? Didi?" My voice was rising,

but I didn't care. "Didi just likes the sound of her own voice. Are other people saying stuff like this?"

"I don't know," Carmen said. She began to laugh nervously, her eyes defensive and pleading. "Please, Martin, I didn't mean to make you upset."

"Well, what did you mean?" I asked. "What did you think was going to happen, coming here and asking me if I'm gay? How did you think I was going to react? God, everything is just one big joke to you, isn't it? Everything is hilarious. Well, I'm not laughing!"

Tears welled up in Carmen's eyes, and my own face felt hot with anger and embarrassment. It was all too much, too fast, too soon. *How am I supposed to answer questions I don't have the answers to? Can everyone just stop asking?*

"I told you not to tell him!" Pickle hissed at Carmen, who swiped at her eyes.

"Well, I thought he'd want to know!" she cried. "Martin, what does it matter? Lots of people are gay!"

"I think *everyone* is probably a *little* gay," Pickle mused aloud.

"I don't want to talk about this," I said, sliding out of the booth. "I've got to go."

"Martin, come on!" Carmen called after me, but I was already bolting down the aisle. A rush of cold autumn air hit my face as I pushed open the door and hurried to my bike, wrestling with the lock. My fingers were shaking too badly to turn the dial, and

I kept missing my numbers.

"Hey, Martin, wait up!" I heard Pickle's voice behind me, but I didn't turn.

"What do you want?" I asked. There was a pang of silence, and I knew he was hurt.

"Carmen means well," he said after a moment. "She just doesn't realize that not everybody's like her. Extroverted, you know."

"Yeah, well, maybe she should do some reflecting on that."

"Yeah," Pickle said, "maybe she should. Listen, I know you and I, we don't talk about our feelings a lot. Or ever. Except for when it comes to Violet, and I'm sorry if I've been obnoxious talking about her. I know that can be annoying."

"You're fine," I said. I took a deep breath to steady my hands and twisted the dial. Finally the lock clicked and opened, and as I slid it off the bike, I turned to Pickle. He had his hands in his pockets, looking forlorn.

"Well," he said, "I just want you to know that I don't care who you like—girl, boy, Mothman." I laughed in spite of myself, and Pickle broke into a relieved smile. "I mean, I might have some questions if you want to date Mothman, like, does he know any other single cryptids? Maybe he could set Carmen up with, say, Bigfoot?"

We laughed, and after I caught my breath, I met Pickle's eye.

"Thanks, Pickle," I said. "Just do me a favor?"

"Of course," Pickle said. "I am eternally at your service."

"If you hear other people at school talking about me . . ."

"They'll be met with the full extent of my verbal wrath," Pickle said, looking gravely serious. "This, I swear to you."

"Thanks," I said. "I should get home."

"Right. I've got to go reassemble Carmen; I'm pretty sure she's a puddle by now."

Pickle clapped me on the shoulder and went back inside the diner. I buckled my helmet and started pedaling home, breathing in deep the cool air.

I've read all about the alternate universe theory, which hypothesizes that there could be infinite universes in existence, where anything and everything is possible. As I pedaled, I wondered what my Alternate Universe Dad would tell Alternate Universe Me about all this. Would he tell me to buck up and pull myself together, or would he hug me and try to talk it out? Would he be on my side? Would he want me to answer that big question, and would the answer matter to him?

Even if I did have an Alternate Universe Dad to talk to, I couldn't imagine putting my feelings into words. I couldn't imagine talking to *anyone* about what I was feeling, actually. I was too jumbled up inside. I didn't want to talk to Mom; I'd get caught in endless circles of feelings and "expression." I didn't want to talk to Tío Billy either. I didn't want to disappoint him by being afraid of who I might be, especially when "who I might be" was so much like him. All I wanted was to close my eyes and suddenly be in another universe, one where my dad decided he wanted me after all—one where I was brave enough, proud enough, loud enough to tell the truth.

★ ★ ★

ReadMe App
OCT. 22—9:45 PM

LadyOfTheStage: Martin?

LadyOfTheStage: Martin, I'm really sorry.

LadyOfTheStage: Please talk to me.

LadyOfTheStage: I didn't know it would upset you so much. Really, I didn't.

LadyOfTheStage: I have to learn to keep my mouth shut sometimes. I know you think everything is a joke to me, but it isn't. I take our friendship seriously. And I'm seriously sorry.

LadyOfTheStage: Martin?

LadyOfTheStage: Okay. Maybe you're not home yet.

LadyOfTheStage: Or maybe you went right to bed.

LadyOfTheStage: I'll try again later and in the morning if I still haven't heard from you.

LadyOfTheStage: I'm sorry. I really am.

☆ 7 ☆

I didn't talk to Carmen for two whole days. Pickle declared himself Switzerland, and swore not to talk to either of us or be our go-between until we made up. When I wasn't working on my drag, I threw myself into Mathletes to distract myself even more. I had to get ready for our after-school study session anyway—the fact that it kept me from thinking about the fight was just a plus.

In a study session, team members can come in and ask each other for help on problems or concepts they don't fully understand yet. I love study sessions, because it's the only place in the universe where I have all the right answers.

"Good afternoon, Martin," Mr. Peterson said as

he breezed into the classroom. I was, as usual, the first one there after the bell rang.

"Hey Mr. P," I replied. "What's new?"

"Oh, you know; same old, same old. Doughnuts in the teacher's lounge today, so that was exciting."

"Old fashioneds?"

"Custard," Mr. Peterson said, pulling a face.

"So not *that* exciting after all," I giggled.

"Precisely."

J.P. and Chris Cregg walked into the room, followed by Poppy and Nelson. Nelson was mid-rant about the cultural importance of Reddit when Chris interrupted him.

"What's up, Mr. P?" he waved cheerily. Mr. Peterson waved back in his usual, semi-awkward fashion.

"Messieurs Cregg and Cregg, good day to you," he said faux-formally. "Poppy, Nelson, welcome."

"Hi," Poppy replied, "and thank you. *Someone* won't stop talking."

"I'm trying to explain to you—"

"You're Nelson-splaining, and I'm bored," she said, plopping down at a desk. "You just like to hear yourself talk." Nelson sighed huffily.

"Whatever," he said. "You'll regret not listening to me when I'm a billionaire e-investor and you're selling your paintings at high school craft fairs."

"At least I'll be selling my art and not selling *out*," she retorted, putting her Converse up on the desk. Mariam came hustling through the door with a stack of books.

"Can you believe the librarian really tried to enforce the checkout limit?" she asked, dumping her pile of tomes next to Poppy. "Like, with me? Of all people? Really?"

Mariam holds the school record for reading comprehension tests. I think she's probably read every book in the school library, twice. J.P. picked up one of Mariam's selections.

"*Marine Biology for Dummies*? Dude, we're landlocked, you know."

"Yes," Mariam replied, looking annoyed as she grabbed the book out of his hands. "But I'm asking for scuba lessons and a new burkini for my birthday. We're going to Maui for spring break and I want to explore shipwrecks for microcosms of the larger marine ecosystem."

"Whatever that means," J.P. scoffed.

"Okay, you all, let's get started," Mr. Peterson said, clapping his hands. "Where's Konrad?"

"Sick," everyone said in unison. Konrad is notorious for getting sick right around Halloween. Actually, he's notorious for getting sick in general. The kid's got the weakest immune system of anyone I've ever met.

"All right then," Mr. Peterson sighed, "I've put worksheets on your desk. Your team captain is your point person for any questions, because I'll be nursing this triple espresso and grading papers." He toasted with his shiny chrome mug and wiggled his eyebrows. "Cheers!"

Everyone got to work, bent over their papers with pencils in hand, but I couldn't focus. My mind was on the triple life I was leading: my friends and Mathletes and drag. My chest was so heavy. *Can I do all of this? Is it even possible? Will I make it out of January intact or as a vaguely Martin-shaped heap of goo?*

"Hey, Martin?" A soft voice interrupted my thought-spiral, and I jumped involuntarily. "Whoa, sorry, I didn't mean to scare you," Chris said. He had sidled up next to me, pulling his chair along.

"It's okay," I said, my hand on my chest. Inside, my heart was racing: *tha-RUMP tha-RUMP tha-RUMP*. I swallowed hard and tried to focus on Chris instead. "What's up?"

"So, I have a question on number six. I'm pretty sure I have to multiply everything by four to get the x coefficients to match up, but I still can't get them to cancel out." Chris shrugged and shook his head, his wispy light brown hair shifting gently to the side. "This is so much more your wheelhouse than mine."

I looked at the problem and right away saw

where he had gone wrong. I took his pencil from his hand and used it to point.

"No. See, you were on track with multiplying by four, but it should have been *negative* four. And you're only multiplying the top equation, because if you multiply everything by negative four, it still won't negate. See what I mean?" I wrote out the next step on his paper, trying to make my chicken-scratch handwriting remotely legible. "Now, $-4x$ and $4x$ cancel out, leaving you with $-13y = 26$, which you can then divide by -13 to get y = -2. Make sense?"

Chris nodded, looking sheepish.

"All I missed was a negative? God, you must think I'm a loser."

"No way!" I exclaimed. "It's an easy mistake to make, especially when you're trying to up your solving speeds."

"Well, thanks," Chris said, taking back his paper. "Um . . ." His eyes fell to his pencil, which was still in my hand.

"Oh! Oh, right. Yes. Here you go." I handed him the pencil, and our fingers brushed. His hand felt warm and a little rough under mine and I remembered that Chris did pottery at the Y in his spare time. Sometimes when Pickle and Carmen and I hang out there, I see him through the window near the climbing wall, coaxing art out of soft lumps of clay.

When I looked up from the page, I could have

sworn he was blushing, the color of summer berries peeking out from under his freckles. I caught his eye, and a jolt of electricity coursed through my stomach.

What was that? I asked myself. *That sort of felt like . . . butterflies.* I couldn't believe Chris Cregg actually thought I was smart enough to help him. He was one of the top students at school, not to mention on the team. As he walked back to his own desk I wondered, just for a second, if maybe Chris would want to hang out sometime, but then my thoughts were interrupted by the snapping of bubblegum behind me.

"Hey, captain?" Poppy asked, her nose scrunched up like a pug's. "This word problem doesn't make any sense. Who in their right mind would buy seven dozen watermelons?"

★ ★ ★

When I checked my phone after practice that night, I had more missed messages from Carmen:

ReadMe App
OCT. 25—5:58 P.M.

LadyOfTheStage: Hi. I know we're still not talking. But I miss you, Martin.
LadyOfTheStage: I swear I didn't mean to upset

you. It's just lately, you've been…well, I guess I just think it's kind of weird.

LadyOfTheStage: I mean, that you would rather hang out with your uncle than hang out with us.

LadyOfTheStage: I'm sure he's really cool and all! But he's like … old. Like, at least 30.

LadyOfTheStage: I'm making this worse, aren't I?

LadyOfTheStage: Martin, pleeeeeease. Pleeeeeease talk to me. I'll do anything to make this better.

LadyOfTheStage: I know I act like I'm above Pickle's antics, but I'm not opposed to bribery and plots in this case!

LadyOfTheStage: Fine, be quiet if you want, but I'm going to find a way to fix this.

LadyOfTheStage: Super-duper, double-dog, mega-extra promise.

I wanted to make up with her; I really did. But I was scared of what she'd say if she knew about Lottie. If she thought hanging out with Tío Billy was weird, what would she think about drag?

It was too much to think about all at once, so instead, I threw myself into Tío Billy's drag queen boot camp.

"Okay, what kind of routine are you thinking?" Tío Billy asked that evening. We were lounging in the living room, where Mom was kneeling on a drop cloth, touching up some leaves on the wall.

Tío Billy was perched on the sofa like a colorful gargoyle, wearing a bright yellow button-down and matching socks. His laptop was on the coffee table with YouTube open.

"I thought we already figured out my routine," I said, confused. "You know, all that walking and posing."

"Well, that's a *type* of routine," he said, "but at the very least, you need music to go with it. Or you could decide to really get dance-y, if you think that's more Lottie's style."

"I think Lottie is a lot like me, only . . . better. More confident, and louder," I said. "I don't think she's a huge dancer. There's no way I could pull off all that choreography," I added, remembering Aida Lott.

"Well, good! 'Cause I ain't no choreographer!" Tío Billy gave a little hoot of laughter. Mom chuckled from her corner and waggled a paintbrush dripping with verdant green in Tío Billy's direction.

"I know that's right!" she said, raising an eyebrow. "He talks a big game, but my little brother couldn't dance his way out of a paper bag, mijo. You sure you don't want me to teach you?"

"Hey, you mind your business, ma'am," Tío Billy shot back. "I've got videos of you at some quinceañeras way back when. I'm sure Martin would *love* to see those!" Mom stuck her tongue out at him, then winked at me and turned back to her painting. Tío Billy started clicking away on his laptop, making a playlist. "We'll keep it to minimal choreo, with a lot of posing, spinning, and serving face."

"Serving face?" I asked.

"It means giving a lot of attitude, a lot of gorgeousness, all in your face. You're *serving* it." Tío Billy demonstrated by shooting me a glamorous look. "Serving it up on a silver platter!"

"I like that," I giggled. I tried to pull a face of my own, but I'm pretty sure I ended up looking like a tropical fish. Tío Billy giggled too.

"We'll work on it!" he said, patting my arm. "So, do you have a song in mind? You'll need something that gives you a lot of confidence and a lot of sparkle. Maybe some Bowie?"

I mumbled in response. Tío Billy raised his eyebrows.

"Uh, I'm sorry, qué dijiste?"

". . . What about Celia Cruz?"

"Ay, a little louder for the people in the back?" He grinned and put his hand up to his ear. "C'mon, I know Miss Lottie León don't whisper! You better own it!"

"Celia Cruz, okay?" I crossed my arms over my chest, pretending to be more offended by his teasing than I actually was. "I like Celia Cruz. She's fun to watch. And her music makes me feel like I can do anything."

"Ooh, yes, Celia!" Mom piped up. "You were

listening to her in the womb, mijo."

"Well, that sounds like exactly what we need!" Tío Billy exclaimed. "There's nothing wrong with a little reina Celia, you know? And salsa, that's a genre that gives us a lot to work with."

"How about 'Yo Viviré'?" I asked tentatively. Tío Billy nodded emphatically.

"A classic!" he crooned, scrolling through YouTube until he found the track. Celia's smooth voice began to play from the speakers, and I started to mimic the maraca players, shaking my fists from side to side. "Wait, wait!" Tío Billy leapt off the couch and went running for the hall closet. He pulled out a massive seafoam colored tutu, plus the box with my silver heels.

"A tutu?" I asked dubiously. Celia warbled in the background as Tío Billy approached, holding the clothes out to me.

"I saw it at the mall and fell in love. If you're going to practice a routine, you better look the part," he said. "Besides, tutus are super hot right now."

The tutu was made of slightly rigid tulle, layers and layers of it, frothing up around an elastic waistband like whipped cream on a B-Town shake.

"Go on," Tío Billy urged, "try it on!"

I wrestled with the waistband a little, then pulled the whole monstrosity on over my pants. I struggled with my T-shirt; it looked boxy and silly hanging out over the tutu, but tucking it in made me look like a doofus. I'd never worn a skirt before, so how would I know how they worked?

"Ay, let me help," Mom said, wiping her hands on her overalls and leaping up to rescue me. "Tuck it in, then pull it out a little. It'll look cool and disheveled, like you don't care about how you look," she advised, showing me how to make the shirt billow slightly at the waist. *Mom's helping,* I thought. *It's funny—she invited Tío Billy to stay with us so I'd have a male influence, but now it's a* female *influence I need.* Mom stepped back to admire her work.

"Does it look okay?" I asked anxiously.

"Ay, que guapo, mi hijo!" Mom nodded. Tío Billy snapped his fingers in my direction, which I took as approval.

"Perfect! Now give us some moves. Show me your walk, with the music," Tío Billy said, restarting the song.

I took a deep breath and closed my eyes, trying to feel the beat of the song. Every limb in my body suddenly felt heavy and awkward, and for more than a moment it was like I had never moved my arms or legs before.

With my eyes shut tight, I tried to imagine what it would be like to be in the audience as Celia performed: the crowd around me constantly moving to the rhythm of the music as if they were a heartbeat personified, *tha-RUMP tha-RUMP tha-RUMP.* I guess my feet started moving of their own accord, because all of a sudden, I was busting out a salsa. A little step to the side, a little shifting of my weight—it couldn't have looked very smooth or very cool, but I was just glad I hadn't fallen over yet.

"There you go!" Tío Billy exclaimed, clasping his hands together in encouragement. "Lottie León is in the house, y'all!" he called to Mom, and she clapped enthusiastically. I caught her eye and grinned, feeling like I was learning to ride a bike all over again: *Look! Look what I can do!*

The music rose up in my chest, and for a second it was like it was me singing instead of Celia. I spun around, enjoying the way the skirt shifted and rose up around me like a cloud. Tío Billy snapped his fingers in the air. "Queen! Yaaas!" he cried.

Celia sang her final notes and I struck a pose, one hand in the air and one on my hip, popped out to one side just like Tío Billy taught me. He jumped to his feet in thunderous applause, whistling and stomping his feet. Mom was hopping up and down, clapping and laughing, her curls bouncing and her smile wide.

And that's when I noticed Carmen.

She was standing on the front stoop, fully visible though the living room window. And she was looking right at me.

I froze.

"Martin?" Mom asked, but I couldn't tear my eyes away from Carmen. I could feel my heart in my stomach, about to pull an *Alien* and burst right out of me.

"What's wrong?" Tío Billy asked. "You were fabulous!"

"I—hold on, I—I have to—Carmen!" I yelled, but she had already turned on her heel and was making her way back down the sidewalk. I tried to shimmy out of the tutu as quickly as I could, but it got caught on my heels and I stumbled and fell. My face flushed hot against the floorboards. I raised myself up on my forearms and knees and kicked off the heels violently.

"León?" I heard the concern in Tío Billy's voice, but I didn't stop. I wrenched open the door and yelled out to Carmen, but she was already at the bottom of the driveway, hopping onto her bike.

"Carmen, wait!" I called and I skidded to a halt in front of her.

"I was coming by to apologize," she said stiffly. "It was going to be a grand gesture. A big, dramatic surprise. But it looks like you've got things covered in the surprise department."

"What you saw—it's—it's not what you think—" I said, gasping. I put my hands on my knees to catch my breath.

"I don't know what I think!" She flailed her arms in the air wildly. "I don't know what this is! Is your uncle making you do this stuff?"

"No!" I exclaimed, my eyes stinging. "It's not like that!"

"It's not *you*, Martin! You were never into anything like this before *he* showed up." She pointed accusatorily at the window. "You've been spending all your time with a relative you see, what, twice a year? And he's turned you into a totally different person! And what's worse is that you didn't feel like you could tell us about it!"

"Well, maybe I would have, if you weren't so busy marrying off Pickle and sucking up to Didi Esposito!" I shot back. I didn't know where that came from, only that I felt totally defenseless. Carmen's mouth dropped open in outrage. She fumbled to buckle her bike helmet under her chin, jamming the pieces together furiously.

"Are you serious? We have always been there for you. When we were talking about you and your uncle the other night, you could have said something then. But instead you just kept on keeping secrets, and now you're here, and you're—you're—you're doing whatever this is!" she spat.

"I didn't know how to bring it up. I didn't know what to say!"

"You *never* know what to say!" she cried. A wave

≥ 123 ≤

of sick, cold shock crashed down on me. There it was. My biggest fault, the thing I wished on the stars nightly to change—and she knew it.

She knew it, and she said it anyway.

"Say something! Say anything!" she shouted. "Don't leave your best friends in the dark like that! All this time I thought something was the matter between us, but instead it was . . . whatever this is? God, I feel so—so—I don't even know what I feel, Martin!"

My ears were ringing, and it felt like my bones were vibrating. I shook my head, trying to clear away the fog of shock and hurt that had settled in my brain.

"I know," I said. "I'm sorry. It's—I'm—it's something I do for fun. Tío Billy showed me when he got here; sometimes he dresses up and lip syncs and, I don't know, it looked like something I could do and maybe be good at."

"You know what you *used* to be good at? Being our friend," she said, crossing her arms over her chest. "What about this is so much better than hanging out with us?"

"It's not," I said, "it's just different. I . . . I like how it makes me feel, okay?" I wanted so badly for her to understand, I was shaking. "It's fun and exciting and sort of silly, and it makes me feel confident and . . . and happy."

Carmen's big eyes softened as her hands steadied her handlebars.

"And being around Pickle and me . . . we don't make you feel that way?" she asked. I'd never heard Carmen's voice so quiet, or so serious. It almost scared me. I stared at my feet.

"I . . . it's not like that . . ." But I couldn't say anything, much less something that would make things right. All my words just disappeared, slipping away to leave my brain simultaneously blank and unbearably loud.

Of course. Of course, this was always the way: Martin McLean with nothing to say. Martin McLean, silent and sheepish and super, super sorry.

"Whatever, Martin," Carmen said, pushing off the driveway and starting to pedal. "Have a nice life with your new best friend. And for the record," she called over her shoulder as she made her way down the sidewalk, "seafoam green isn't your color!"

I would have laughed, if her words hadn't knocked the wind from my lungs.

My chest felt as though someone had punched me repeatedly. I don't know at what point the tears started flowing, but the next thing I knew I was sobbing, bent over myself, about to be sick. The front door opened and Tío Billy's hand was on my shoulder and Mom was saying something, but I couldn't make any of it out. All I could hear was the rushing in my ears and my ugly gasps for air and Carmen's voice echoing in my head.

I felt them pull me up off the ground and help me inside, and then the awful white noise in my quiet-loud head drowned everything, *everything* out.

☆ 8 ☆

After I recovered—after waking up in my bed and crying some more, and after several mugs of Tío Billy's magic hot chocolate—I knew what I had to do. So on Halloween morning, I pedaled my bike over to Carmen's. It was extraordinarily cold for an October day, even for Indiana. The leaves had almost completely fallen, leaving the trees bare. I imagined them shivering in the blustery wind as I rode.

Inside, I was shivering too. I felt as though I'd had a chill ever since that day in the driveway. It was Carmen's voice that did it, so cold and so . . . hurt. It reminded me of Mom, when Dad used to yell at her. When I yelled at her. I knew that keeping secrets from Carmen and Pickle wasn't right. It wasn't, and yet . . . wasn't Lottie my secret to keep or to tell?

Nobody tells you how to know, you know? What parts of you to share, what parts of you to hide. I had to hope that Carmen would accept me—and Lottie—because I needed her to. If my friends couldn't love all the different parts of me, even the ones that answered to a different name, that would be worse than a thousand terrible fights.

I got to Carmen's house and rang the doorbell. Then I waited, riddled with anxiety, until her face appeared in the window.

"Hey," I said weakly when she opened the door. I kept my icy hands planted firmly in my pockets.

"Hi," Carmen said, her eyes looking over me warily. She was already in full costume as Captain Hook, and she looked ridiculous, in the best way. She had a huge maroon hat done up in velvet with a big turquoise plume stuck in it, plus a thick, wavy wig that looked like something from a Renaissance painting. A bushy, curled black mustache was stuck above her upper lip, and peeking out from the lacy cuffs of her matching velvet coat was a silver hook.

"You look great," I said. She shrugged and was silent. I took a deep breath. "Carmen, I'm really sorry."

"For what?"

"Everything," I gushed. "So much. I'm sorry for freaking out at you at the diner, and I'm sorry I didn't tell you about Lottie."

"Lottie?"

My voice caught in my throat. Saying Lottie's name aloud to someone other than Mom or Tío Billy . . . it made her real. And if Carmen rejected Lottie— rejected *me*—I might as well start looking for a new school. But I had to tell her. I had to, because she mattered to me. Carmen, and Lottie too.

"That's my stage name," I said, trying to ignore how my voice shook. "My drag name. Well, sort of. It will be! Not yet, though. I'm sort of in training," I said. Carmen's mouth was hanging open, but she didn't say anything. "I go by Lottie León. Or, I will, if I ever actually perform."

"So . . . you're a drag queen?" she asked.

I nodded.

"But . . . wait . . . does this mean . . . ?"

Does this mean you're gay?

She didn't have to say it. I knew what she was asking. I felt that familiar beating in my chest as my heart took off flying. I took a deep breath and remembered what Tío Billy said: it's okay not to know.

"I don't know," I admitted. "I just know I like being Lottie."

Carmen shifted uncomfortably, and I could see her thinking hard behind her gigantic hat. Then she sighed, and her eyes met mine.

"I'm not going to lie," she began, and my

stomach dropped to my toes. "I'm still getting used to this new you, Martin. It's just . . . this is a lot of new information."

"For me too," I said. "I didn't know anything about drag until Tío Billy took me to a show. But it was so amazing, Carmen; you would love it. It's kind of like going to the theater! There's so much color and music and glitter, and the outfits . . ." I trailed off, because Carmen was looking at me strangely. "What?"

"If you think I'd like it so much," she said, "why did you hide it from me?"

"I guess . . . I love you a lot, Carmen. I know we don't really say that stuff to each other, but it's true. You and Pickle are the closest thing I have to real siblings. But now I love drag, too, and . . . I was scared that you would hate it, or hate me, or both. And that would hurt my heart too much." I had never talked about my feelings in front of Carmen before. It felt like walking a tightrope over the Grand Canyon in my underpants—totally vulnerable and majorly scary. I braced myself for her response.

"Well . . . it's going to be a little weird to me for a while. But . . ." Carmen's big, earnest eyes met my gaze. "You're my best friend, Martin, and if this is something you love, then I can learn to love it too."

"Really?"

"Yeah." Carmen smiled. "It *does* sound like something I'd like. You're talking to a girl in a mustache, after all." I giggled. "And I'm really sorry for the awful things I said, Martin. I was surprised and confused, and it came out as anger. I didn't mean to—"

"I know," I reassured her. "It's okay."

Then Carmen let out a high-pitched little noise, so shrill it made Woofecito start barking up a storm, and pulled me into a hug.

"Oh, Martin," she said into my shoulder. "I'm so glad to have you back." When we pulled apart, her fake mustache was a little wet with tears. "And I want you to know," she said, wiping her nose, "I'm not going to bring up the 'G' word anymore, because it's none of my business. Okay?"

"Thanks, Carmen," I said, suddenly sort of bashful.

"Have you told Pickle yet?" she asked. "About Lottie?"

"Not yet," I said. "I was waiting for the right time."

"You know," she said, toying with the hem of her pirate's coat. "After you left B-Town the other night, we sort of talked about it."

"About what?"

"About how we'd feel if you, you know . . . *were*. The 'G' word, I mean. I know, I'm sorry, I know I just said I wouldn't bring it up, but listen! We both said, without hesitation, that we'd love you just the same. Well," she stopped herself momentarily, "Pickle didn't use the word 'love,' because he's Pickle and he only ever says that to Violet, but the sentiment was the same. And I think that probably applies to you being a drag queen too."

"Wait," I said, "Pickle told Violet he loves her?"

Carmen looked horrified and clamped her non-hook hand over her mouth.

"Oh nooo," she cried. "I promised not to tell!"

"Why?"

"Because he was worried you'd make fun of him!"

"Me? This paragon of tenderness standing before you?" I gestured to myself and my puffy winter coat. Carmen giggled. "No way. I think it's pretty sweet, actually."

"It really is. They look at each other all goonie-eyed all throughout lunch. Violet's actually been hanging out with us a lot lately," she said.

"Wow," I said, "I've missed so much." I'd been eating my lunches in the library, even though we're definitely not supposed to. I had to hide my sandwich from the librarian when she came by.

"You have," Carmen said. "But you don't have to keep missing stuff, you know."

"Yeah. I know. Are we okay?"

"Yes," she said. "Definitely."

"Promise?" I asked. Carmen rolled her eyes at me.

"Super-duper, double-dog, mega-awesome promise."

"With sprinkles on top?"

"With sprinkles on top," she grinned.

"Good. Oh, hey! I wanted to show you something." I unzipped my coat and dramatically ripped it open at my chest, like Superman.

"Oh my gosh!" Carmen said, pretending to swoon. I had dressed as Tinkerbell for her, for the group costume. Okay, so it wasn't *exactly* a Tinkerbell costume in the traditional sense. It wasn't a dress—I wasn't ready for that, yet—but it was a Tink-green T-shirt, khakis, and lime green kicks that I had tied little white puffs to, just like Tinkerbell's shoes. Tío Billy had helped me make a light-up magic wand out of glow sticks, and I wore a lime green beanie instead of Tinkerbell's ribbons.

"You're like a cool, hipster Tinkerbell!" Carmen cried. "You're Tinker Bro!"

"Thank you, thank you," I said, bowing.

"What made you change your mind?" Carmen asked. "You know, about the costume?" I shrugged.

"If dressing up as a group makes you as happy as drag makes me, then that's something I want to do, you know?" I said. Carmen looked like she might cry.

"I've really missed you, Martin," she said.

"I've really missed you too," I said. And I meant it.

Carmen and I caught the bus near her house and just barely made it to school on time. We met up with Pickle and Violet during lunch, sitting at our usual table near the front of the cafeteria. Pickle was dressed up as Peter Pan, as promised, with the tights and everything. Violet was wearing Wendy Darling's nightgown costume from the Disney movie, only instead of a blue dress, she had made her own version in a light purple with a matching bow. Sparkly streamers were attached to the back of her wheelchair, below a sign that read "POWERED BY PIXIE DUST." The four of us looked awesome together, I had to admit.

"Looks like the two of you have decided to call off the Cold War," Pickle said as Carmen and I sat down with our lunch trays. "Have we returned to our regularly scheduled programming?"

"We have!" Carmen replied in a chipper tone. Her eyes fell to a piece of Halloween-themed cake on Violet's tray. "Ooh, where did you get that?"

"Over by the milk and stuff," Violet said, gesturing with her fork. "It's way good. Here, I'll show you where it is." She blew a kiss at Pickle and set out with Carmen in pursuit of cake. Pickle leaned toward me over the table.

"So what happened with you guys anyway?" he asked, smearing a French fry through some ketchup. "Carmen was so upset the other night, she wouldn't even talk about it. And that girl *loves* to talk."

So Carmen didn't tell Pickle what she saw. I looked around the cafeteria and lowered my voice.

"She sort of . . . look, if I tell you this, do you promise you won't blab?"

"Moi?" Pickle asked, feigning total disbelief. "I am a rock, baby. I'm a fortress."

"Okay, because it's kind of big."

"Go on," he said, raising an eyebrow at me. I cleared my throat nervously.

"She came by the other night and she . . . saw me dressed up," I said, watching Pickle's face.

"Like, red carpet, penguin suit dressed up? Or like mascot dressed up?"

"No, like . . . *dressed* up. Like, in a dress. Well, a skirt, technically."

"A skirt," he repeated, with no inflection. I nodded. "What the devil do you mean, McLean?"

"I . . . I do drag," I whispered, trying to keep him from making some kind of scene. You never knew with Pickle. "I'm a drag queen."

Pickle considered this, his face rumpled in contemplation. I braced myself for any number of uncomfortable questions: *So does that mean you're gay? Do you like boys now? Do you want to be a girl?*

He chomped thoughtfully on a fry and asked, "Are you any good?"

I blinked.

"Um," I said, "I don't know. I'm sort of still learning. But there's an all-ages competition coming up, and my uncle's helping me."

"What do you get if you win?"

"A thousand dollars," I said.

Pickle dropped his fry. "A THOUSAND DOLLARS?" he yelled, leaping to his feet in excitement.

"Sit! Down!" I hissed, waving at him like an idiot and turning eleven shades of red. Slow as a parade float, he lowered himself back into his seat with dignity, but his face was still bug-eyed.

"Martin. Martin, Martin, Martin," he repeated, tenting his fingers like a yoga guru. "Martin, my dude, this seals it. You are officially my coolest friend."

"What are you talking about?"

"I don't know anybody doing anything as hardcore as this! You're going to put on those pointy, pinchy shoes girls wear, and those amazing clothes, and dance around all night, and then somehow when you're still standing afterward you're gonna win *one thousand freaking dollars*!" he said. "That's awesome!"

"I'm . . . thanks, Pickle," I said, still shaking off the shock.

"What are we talking about?" Carmen asked, approaching with two hands full of cake.

"Oh, you know, Martin's a drag queen and he's gonna be filthy rich," Pickle replied. I choked on my milk.

"Pickle!" I cried, looking from Violet to him and back again.

"It's cool," he replied, cocking his head at Violet. "She's cool."

Violet serenely glided up to the table and parked herself at the head. She seemed totally unfazed by Pickle's comments.

"Hi, Martin," she said. "It's good to see you. I feel like it's been ages."

"Hi, yeah," I said. "How are you?"

"Oh, fine," she said, tossing her long black hair over her shoulder. "Just trying to convince Peter to come out trick-or-treating with me tonight."

I raised an eyebrow in Pickle's direction as Carmen tittered away next to me. Pickle looked like he wanted to sink into the ground.

"Peter?" I asked.

"Yes," Pickle said through gritted teeth, "how can I help you, dearest Martin?"

"I'm sorry, I'm looking for my friend Pickle. Do you know where I can find him?"

Violet giggled and patted Pickle's hand. "I know he doesn't like that I call him Peter," Violet said. "But how am I supposed to introduce him to my family tonight? 'Mom, Dad, this is my boyfriend *Pickle*.'" She shook her head.

"Pickle is a Jewish name, isn't it?" I grinned at him before shoveling salad into my mouth. Pickle shot daggers at me with his eyes.

"Martin is Spanish for 'a very rude guy,' right?"

he replied. I pretended to clutch my heart in pain. "And anyway," Pickle said to Violet, "don't be so sure that you'll be introducing me to them tonight." He turned to Carmen and me. "She has four younger brothers and sisters. I'm going to be taken down by an army of children!"

"You are not," Violet chided. "It's going to be fine."

"Are all your siblings adopted, too?" Carmen asked. Pickle blanched.

"Carmen!" he hissed. "You cannot! Just ask people! If they are adopted!"

"Well, it's not like they're here," Carmen said, blithely swinging a forkful of cake in his direction.

Violet laughed good-naturedly. "Peter, it's okay," she said, putting a hand on Pickle's arm. "Yes, they're all adopted through an agency in Hanoi, like me."

"But you're not like, *related*-related, right?"

"They're my brothers and sisters," Violet said firmly. Carmen blushed. "But, no, we're not related by blood. I was adopted first, then Leah a few years later, then the twins, then Elijah," Violet continued, scraping remnants of frosting off her plate. "Honestly, if you saw how we act when we're together you'd see that we're really no different from biological siblings. It's true that we don't look like our parents—or even quite like each other—but the way we all bicker and make up over and over again, we're *definitely* family."

Just then, Nelson passed by the table, holding his lunch tray. He was dressed as Kylo Ren, but he had the mask pushed back on his head. He noticed us and sneered.

"Well, look at this," he said, hovering on Violet's side of the table. "If it isn't the Three Musket-queers." He turned his gaze to Violet. "And I see you've found a mascot to wheel out when you want to look extra pathetic."

"Hey!" Pickle cried, standing up.

"That's an awful thing to say," Violet said, looking as though she might spit in Nelson's face.

"Oh, is it? I had no idea," he mocked. Then he looked at me, and I felt my insides turn to ice. "Good to see you haunting the loser table again, McLean the Queen. Or should I say, Twink-erbell," he snorted. "Off to sprinkle some fairy dust?"

"Shut up, Nelson," I said, but it came out so quietly I could barely hear myself. Behind Nelson, Chris Cregg was approaching. His good-natured smile faded when he saw the look on my face. Recognition appeared in Chris's blue eyes.

"Nelson," Chris said as he made it to our table, "Mr. Peterson was looking for you."

"Why?" Nelson said, curling his lip.

Chris scratched the back of his neck and shrugged. "I don't know. I just ran into him," he replied. "He said something about suspending you from the team? Something about a formal report of bullying?"

All the blood drained from Nelson's face. Everyone at the table was silent, watching him.

"You're—you're lying," he stammered, trying to keep his composure. Chris shook his head sadly.

"Why would I lie? If you get suspended, we're totally screwed. I don't know, man, I would go find him ASAP."

Nelson looked from me to Chris to Pickle, then back to Chris. He grumbled something unintelligible—I caught the word "nerds"—and shuffled off in a huff. I turned to Chris in awe.

"That was amazing!" I said. "How'd you come up with that?"

"It was easy," Chris shrugged. "Nelson knows he's a jerk. Couldn't be hard to convince him other people thought so too."

"Have you ever considered trying out for Drama?" Carmen probed, sliding over to make space between us at the table. She patted the open seat, and Chris sat down. "We could really use someone with your improv abilities."

"Uh, no, I haven't," Chris laughed, "but maybe I will!" We were smushed pretty close together on the bench. Chris turned to me. "I wasn't lying about running into Mr. Peterson, though. He caught me in the hall—we qualified for Regionals!"

"Really?" *Yes! Regionals!* I thought, and then: *Oh, no. Regionals. Regionals and All-Ages Night. It's happening. It's really happening!*

"Yes, really!" Chris said with a laugh. "As if there were any doubt, with you at the podium."

"Wow. Thanks. I . . . wow," I stammered, but Chris was too busy looking at my outfit to notice that I wasn't exactly over the moon about the news.

"Great costume," he said. "What are you supposed to be?"

"Um, I'm sort of supposed to be Tinkerbell," I mumbled into my tray. "I guess kind of a hipster Tinkerbell? For the group costume." I gestured vaguely to the group. Chris nodded.

"Awesome! I was gonna guess Jughead. You know, from the Archie comics? With the beanie, you look kinda like him. . . ." Chris gestured to his own head and then blushed, illuminating his freckles with that sunrise glow. "Anyway, I like it."

"Hey, I know who you're supposed to be," I said, really looking at Chris for the first time since he'd broken the news about Regionals. He was wearing a black T-shirt with a dark blue symbol on it, black pants, and a black mask covering his eyes, and he was carrying two cardboard paper towel rolls painted black.

"You do?" he blinked.

"You're Nightwing!" I said. "Also known as—"

"Dick Grayson!" Chris exclaimed, looking surprised. "I thought I was the only one I knew who liked comics!"

"No way, I'm obsessed!"

"Wow," Pickle said, casting a dubious look at Carmen and Violet. "Are we about to be replaced?" I made a face at him.

"Yeah, our older brother Matthew-John left J.P. and me a bunch of comics when he went off to college. J.P. never really got into them." Chris shrugged. "More for me, right?"

"Totally," I said. "What's your favorite series?" Chris mulled on that for a second, drumming his freckled, calloused fingers against the table.

"Hmm. I actually really like the *Batman: Detective* comics they're doing in the Rebirth series," he mused, "but I've also been kind of into the comics they're doing with *Overwatch*." He looked shyly down at his shoes. "I know that's super geeky."

"What? No way!" I cried. "I love *Overwatch*!"

"Seriously?" Chris grinned. "Who do you main?"

"McCree," I replied. "You?"

"D.Va. I wish I had her mech in real life!"

"Me too!"

"You know," he whispered, "I heard Nelson mains Junkrat."

I rolled my eyes. "Figures," I said. "The resemblance is uncanny."

We dissolved into laughter. Chris actually got

a cramp in his stomach, he was laughing so hard. Soon we all settled into comfortable chatter together, Pickle taking bets on which of Violet's younger siblings would inflict bodily harm on him first. But while the rest of them talked, I was only half listening. *Two competitions, one night, and one very nervous Martin,* I thought. *I need a plan.*

But then there was Chris. His presence at the lunch table kept me from fully disappearing into problem-solving mode. *He's never sat with us before,* I thought. *Could it be that he'd actually be my friend outside of Mathletes?* It seemed like an impossibility, and yet, when the lunch bell rang and we went to put our trays away, I was struck with a sudden wave of confidence. I caught up with Chris by the tray return station.

"Hey, would you ever want to come over and play video games sometime?" I asked, bracing myself for instant regret. *Chris Cregg is way,* way *more popular than I'll ever be. Why would he want to hang out with me after school?* I watched his face for embarrassment or disgust, but instead, Chris nodded enthusiastically.

"Yeah, sure! We'll plan something soon," he said, holding out his knuckles for me to bump.

"I—uh—yeah! We will! Thanks!" I said, tripping over myself to tap his knuckles. He smiled and waved goodbye, heading for his next class. Pickle sidled up next to me before I had a chance to process what had just happened.

"Dude, what's your deal?"

"What do you mean?" I asked. "My deal? With Chris? I don't have a deal."

"Uh, okay," Pickle said sarcastically. "He told you you're going to Regionals, but you acted like he said you're overdue for a visit to the dentist! Regionals, dude! I thought you'd be doing cartwheels across the cafeteria, but you were totally zoned out for the rest of lunch."

"I know," I said. "But there's a problem. Regionals is the same night as the drag competition."

"Hmm," Pickle said, stroking an invisible beard on his chin. "This sounds like the perfect time for one of my Patented Pickle Plans."

A Patented Pickle Plan is just another name for one of Pickle's ridiculous hijinks. He came up with the name on the playground in fourth grade, and it stuck. Once he devised a Patented Pickle Plan to build a clubhouse in the patch of woods behind his house. He ended up having to go to the hospital after accidentally stepping on a piece of plywood he left nail-side up. That is pretty typical of a Patented Pickle Plan.

"Oh, no," I groaned. "I'm not sure a Patented Pickle Plan is what we need."

"Ouch! You wound me!" Pickle replied.

"We can talk about it later," I said. "Say *nothing* to Chris!"

"About this, specifically? Or can I not say

anything to him at all? Because it might be a little rude if I—"

"Pickle!"

"Sorry, sorry. Serious now!" he said. "For what it's worth, dude, I don't really talk to Chris, so your secret is safe with me."

"Thanks," I replied. "I'm just . . . not sure I'm ready for the Mathletes to know about the whole drag thing."

Pickle nodded sagely. "I shall take this knowledge to my grave, if that is what my liege requires," he said in a bad English accent. "Hark, math class awaits!" Pickle bowed deeply and headed off toward Mr. Peterson's classroom.

Pickle and Carmen know that I do drag, I thought happily, watching Pickle walk away, *and they actually think it's kind of cool!* So maybe it didn't matter that Nelson was a bully, or that I had no idea how I would do both Regionals and All-Ages Night. Maybe, despite all that, everything would be all right. It was as though the ever-expanding universe had stopped, just for a minute, and let me spin in my own orbit, where everything was just as it should be.

Carmen came up next to me, shaking her head in wonder.

"I can't believe one of the popular kids sat with us," she said. "Didi Esposito is going to *freak*!"

NOVEMBER & DECEMBER

ReadMe App
NOV. 3—4:07 PM

PicknLittle: Hear ye, hear ye!

LadyOfTheStage: What now, Pickle?

mathletesmartin: Shh, he's making a proclamation.

LadyOfTheStage: ...I want you both to know I am rolling my eyes LOUDLY.

mathletesmartin: That's an impressive trick.

PicknLittle: AHEM

LadyOfTheStage: All right, okay, go on

PicknLittle: We are gathered here today to discuss an item on the agenda, the issue of one Martin Reginald McLean!

mathletesmartin: My middle name is *not* Reginald

PicknLittle: MARTIN REGINALD MCLEAN, and the conflicting times of his Junior Mathletes competition and his drag show. It is up to us, as best friends, to solve said issue.

mathletesmartin: Up to you?!

PicknLittle: Are we not the Three Musketeers?

mathletesmartin: Of course we are

PicknLittle: And are we not all for one, one for all?

LadyOfTheStage: Always

PicknLittle: Then we'll figure it out, because there's nothing the Three Musketeers can't do!

LadyOfTheStage: Hear, hear!

mathletesmartin: Any ideas, then?

PicknLittle: …

LadyOfTheStage: …

mathletesmartin: …

LadyOfTheStage: Okay, so maybe we take some time to think about it?

mathletesmartin: Seems that way.

PicknLittle: Can I ask Violet if she has any ideas?

LadyOfTheStage: Martin?

mathletesmartin: Um, I guess so. She didn't seem bothered by it at all when it came up at lunch.

PicknLittle: I know, right? She's pretty much the best.

LadyOfTheStage: Aw, that's sweet

PicknLittle: I LOVE HER SO MUCH, YOU GUYS.

mathletesmartin: So yeah, you can ask her. But you have to swear her to secrecy! I'm not ready for the whole school to know about this.

LadyOfTheStage: Yes, make her swear and prick her thumb and hold it against a Bible, or something.

PicknLittle: She's Jewish

LadyOfTheStage: Well, the Torah then, I don't know!

PicknLittle: Got it

PicknLittle: Hey, Martin?

mathletesmartin: ?

PicknLittle: Thanks for telling us. I promise not to

ask too many silly questions.

mathletesmartin: Really?

PicknLittle: No, of course not, Martin Reginald. Silly questions are *my* middle name.

LadyOfTheStage: Ah yes, Pickle "Silly Questions" Tufts.

PicknLittle: I...did not think that through.

mathletesmartin: You guys are awesome. Seriously.

LadyOfTheStage: Right back atcha.

☆ **9** ☆

By November, it had become apparent that I needed an outfit to wear for All-Ages Night. Tío Billy called this my "look" and said that any drag queen worth her fake eyelashes had a signature style that defined her. We set to scouring every nearby thrift store for ideas, but there were so many options, it made my head spin.

"What about this one?" I asked, pulling a long black dress off a rack. The local Goodwill was decked out in Thanksgiving decorations, with paper turkeys taped on all the dressing room doors and jewel-toned leaves hanging on the walls like garland. Tío Billy felt the sleeve and wrinkled his nose.

"Ay, no way. That's wool. You'll burn up under the stage lights in that." He flipped through a few more dresses before selecting one that slipped through his fingers like silk. "See? Much better. Sure, it's not the most expensive fabric in the world, but at least you won't sweat your makeup off!"

"It's nice," I said, feeling the hem between my fingers, "but I'm not sure it's quite 'Lottie' enough, you know?"

"Then we keep looking!" Tío Billy declared, putting the dress back on the rack. I flipped through a few more hangers halfheartedly. Tío Billy looked at me out of the corner of his eye as he examined a floral dress that flowed all the way down to the floor. "Que bola, león?"

"I wish I had a picture in my head of what she looks like," I said. "When I close my eyes and imagine Lottie up on stage, it's . . . more of a feeling than an image."

"Describe the feeling, then," Tío Billy said, absentmindedly shaking his head at a lime green, halter-neck prom dress. "What does being Lottie *feel* like?"

I closed my eyes and pictured the stage at Hoosier Mama. Instead of being Lottie, I was watching her, outside my body but feeling everything she felt. *Electricity. The color magenta. Pineapple soda bubbles dissolving on the tongue. Glitter and brass. Carmen's laugh, and Pickle's grin, and Chris's eyes—*

A warm flush bloomed in my cheeks. I peeked, and Tío Billy was watching me.

"I don't know," I said quickly. "It feels like . . . a victory. A celebration."

"Oh, so she's a party queen, huh?" Tío Billy said, ribbing me with his elbow. I shrugged.

"She's the version of me that can sing and dance like Celia Cruz," I said, "and own the stage like Cassie Blanca."

"Now *that* is the sweetest thing I've ever heard!" he exclaimed. His face lit up as he reached into the depths of the clothing racks. "Speaking of Celia Cruz . . ." he said, and pulled out a shimmering hot pink minidress covered in hundreds of strands of tiny beads. "Doesn't this remind you of her hair in the 'Yo Viviré' video? That gorgeous little bob?"

I ran my hands over the dress, feeling the beading move beneath my fingers as if it were alive. The color seemed to change in the light, shifting in an instant from a barely-there whisper of pink to an explosion of fuchsia.

And all I once I could see Lottie, really *see* her. I couldn't explain it if I tried—it was as though she just popped into my brain, fully formed and fabulous and wearing that dress.

"It's awfully heavy," Tío Billy said hesitantly, watching my eyes pore over every inch of the dress. "It might weigh you down too much on stage."

"It's perfect," I whispered. Tío Billy seemed surprised.

"It *is* a great little number," he reasoned. "Are you sure, león? This is the one?"

I nodded, without looking up at him. In my hands, the beads sparkled like infinite stars.

"It's *perfect*."

★ ★ ★

That afternoon, Mom had me stand on an overturned paint bucket so she could start some alterations to the dress. It *was* heavy, like Tío Billy said, but I liked that it forced me to be aware of how I moved in it. It made me feel more like Lottie. The dress was just a little too big in the waist and hips, though Mom assured me she could take it in. From up on my makeshift pedestal, I watched her work with fascination. *Before Lottie, I didn't even know Mom could sew,* I thought as she pinned my right side. *Who would have thought we'd bond over drag, of all things?*

"When did you get so tall, mijo?" she asked. I shrugged.

"He's eating his Wheaties, Gena!" Tío Billy called from the kitchen. He poked his head into the living room, chomping on a pastelito de guayaba we picked up from the Cuban bakery on our way home.

"I'll say!" Mom exclaimed, shifting over to pin my opposite side. "So is your outfit finished now?"

"Nope," I shook my head. "We're still missing a jacket." I had decided to go all-out evoking Celia in the "Yo Viviré" video, which meant including a square-shouldered jacket that Tío Billy assured me we could make "fashion." Part of me wished I had a bata cubana, the type of dress Celia was famous for wearing, but there aren't exactly a lot of those lying around the thrift stores of southern Indiana. But with a little creativity, I knew I could channel Celia in my own way—in Lottie's way.

"What kind?" she asked. Tío Billy brushed the crumbs off his face and hands so he could pull up a photo on his phone.

"It's sort of dark, but it's also covered in big jewels or sequins or something, so it's sparkly. I know it's kind of ugly" I admitted as she glanced at Tío Billy's screen, "but it really does make the whole outfit."

"Not ugly, león. Camp!"

"I think I had something like that back in the day," Mom said. Tío Billy snorted and pulled a face. "Hey!" she yelped. "It was de moda back then, I'll have you know!"

"Oh, sure," Tío Billy said as I giggled. "You keep telling yourself that!"

"Don't listen to him, Martin," Mom said. "But if you're looking for clothes, you can check the attic. All my old stuff is up there."

"Thank God," Tío Billy said, pretending to whisper to me. Mom rolled her eyes, then stood and patted my arm.

"All done pinning, mijo." I hopped off the paint bucket and shimmied out of the dress, which Mom carefully folded over her arm. "Why don't you go up and look for that jacket now? I'll get to work taking this in," she said, placing a kiss on my cheek.

"C'mon, león, I'll help you look," Tío Billy said, heading for the stairs.

The last time I went up to the attic, it was right after Dad left. I was helping Mom pack up things that reminded her of him. I was so mad about having to help. I thought for sure he'd be back any minute, and then we'd have packed all those boxes for nothing. But when you're six, I guess you get to be wrong about that kind of stuff.

Tío Billy pulled down the ladder to the attic, allowing me to scurry up with him close behind. At the top, I hoisted myself onto the floor and scanned the cramped space. There were garbage bags full of old clothes and piles of toys that I hadn't touched in years.

"Good grief," Tío Billy said, looking around. "Hasn't your mom ever heard of a garage sale?"

"She's too busy to have one," I said, kicking aside a bag of old bed linens. "When Dad left, she went on a cleaning spree. It was easier to pack all the junk away than figure out what to do with it."

"Out of sight, out of mind," Tío Billy murmured, tentatively opening a clear plastic bin. It was stuffed with Mom-wear—paisley capris and maternity clothes, colorful caftans and various fringed items. We dove in, laughing and cringing at some of the old fashions. At the very bottom of the whole mess I found a cropped jacket with long sleeves, the lapels weighed down with tons and tons of huge jewels. *Bingo*.

"Well, I don't know if la reina Celia would wear it, but we're doing things a la Lottie!" Tío Billy said briskly, replacing the lid on the bin. I was ready to head back downstairs and show off my findings to Mom, but something caught my eye in the corner of the room. Behind a long-forgotten hula hoop and two pairs of inline skates, there stood a worn and sunken pyramid of boxes labeled "KEVIN'S STUFF." I went over and ran my hand across the dusty top box. *What else did he leave behind?* I tore the tape seal off the cardboard flaps and looked inside.

The contents of the box were cushioned with his old shirts, a thick green flannel that smelled very faintly of his shaving cream, and a super soft T-shirt with Captain America's shield on it. An old video camera was wrapped up inside them, a big bulky thing with an ugly black strap and a bunch of cords nestled around it. I lifted it up and turned it over in my hands.

"What'd you find?" Tío Billy asked, coming over with the jacket slung over his shoulder. I found a little screen on the side of the camera and flipped it open. The screen flashed bright blue for a split second, then displayed a "No Battery" symbol. "Ah," he said, clucking his tongue. "Dios, your dad was never without one of those."

"It's dead," I said, disappointed. Tío Billy picked up the nest of cords and began untangling them.

"I'm willing to bet one of these charges that bad boy," he said, wrestling with a knot. "Should be easy enough."

We took our findings downstairs and started charging the camera. Later, when it had enough juice to turn on, I unplugged it and darted up to my room.

I shut the door behind me and immediately flipped open the camera. A green light flashed steadily on the side of the device, and a menu appeared on the screen: "FILM. LIBRARY. DELETE." I clicked "LIBRARY" and the screen changed to a bunch of thumbnails. Most of them looked like still photos of Mom, but one of them looked like it was a picture of a baby. I used the little arrow buttons on the camera to get over to that thumbnail, and clicked.

An hourglass symbol appeared, dancing back and forth, and then a video started playing. It was in our first house, a little bungalow on the other side of town near where the students lived. Mom was standing in the background, stirring something on the stove. She was so young, with her hair spilling down to the middle of her back in beautiful curls, and a red flower pinned behind her ear. Music played in the background as the camera turned quickly from Mom to a baby, maybe a year and a half old, in front of the beat-up gray-blue couch we'd had forever.

There I was, in all my pudgy baby glory, standing in a diaper and a pair of Mom's red patent leather pumps with a small heel. I wore big black sunglasses that took up half my face and had a purple feather boa wrapped around my shoulders. Little plastic jewels were stuck haphazardly to my earlobes. I was laughing, the sunglasses drooping down off my nose, and wriggling my little baby butt to the music.

"Go Martin! Go Martin!" said a deep voice from the other side of the camera. A pale arm, covered in downy reddish hairs, reached out and fixed the sunglasses with a chuckle. The hand rustled my hair, a tiny Afro bouncing to the beat. "Gena, he looks just like you when you dance!"

"Oh, shut up!" Mom scolded from the kitchen.

"I'm just kidding, Martin. Your mother is a great dancer."

"That's much better!" Mom called. Baby me squealed in delight at hearing Mom's voice, clapping my hands and stomping my feet in her heels. All of a sudden, my foot fell out of the shoe, and I started to tumble.

"Whoa, there, big guy!" Dad reached out and steadied me, setting the camera aside momentarily to pick me up. The camera focused instead on Minxy, the black and white cat we used to have. Dad took her with him when he left. I wondered how she was doing, if she was okay. I hoped Dad's new kids were nice to her.

When he picked the camera back up, it was facing him, with me in his arms. He wore a striped tank top and wire-rimmed glasses, his strawberry blond hair falling into his eyes. He was young, with stubble on his chin and a sparkle in his eye. Dad held the camera out with one hand and kept me hoisted up with the other.

"Listen," he said to the camera, "This is all fun and games now, but you had better grow out of this. I don't know how I could live with a son who likes dresses and heels." And he grinned.

"Kevin!" Mom scolded from the kitchen, but Dad just laughed.

"What? It's true! All those gays in the film department with me think they're God's gift to the art form."

He set me down on the floor and placed the camera next to me. A pair of feet in striped socks went padding into the kitchen, and the camera caught a glimpse of Dad putting his arms around Mom.

"You know Billy is . . ." I heard Mom say, but the rest was drowned out by baby me picking up the camera. The lens turned on my face: a gummy smile, a burst of purple feathers, a flash of jewel-tone sparkled from the stickers on my ears.

"Uh-uh-uh, no way, buddy, that camera costs more than this house!" Dad said, rushing over to pry it out of my hands. There was a jumbling of images as he reached for the camera, a swirling of faces: his, mine, Mom's in the background. The final frame was me, so small and helpless, looking to him, in my heels, on the ground.

The video ended. A sudden, empty silence filled the room. The LIBRARY screen reappeared in a harsh burst of white light.

And then I was alone on my bed, wondering how words said so long ago by someone gone for so long could hurt so bad.

I set the camera down and cried.

★ ★ ★

ReadMe App
DEC. 19—12:01 P.M.

vividviolet: Helloooooo?
vividviolet: Anybody?
mathletesmartin: Hey, Violet
mathletesmartin: Happy Hanukkah!
vividviolet: Thanks! Where is everybody?
mathletesmartin: What do you mean?

vividviolet: I thought Carmen had planned a brainstorming session for noon...?

mathletesmartin: Oh, yeah, she ended up pushing it back to 3, cause she wanted to go caroling with the madrigal singers.

vividviolet: Well, now I'm embarrassed

mathletesmartin: Pickle forgot to tell you?

vividviolet: Totally

mathletesmartin: Yikes. I'm sorry

vividviolet: Oh, that's all right. It just means I get more time to chat with you!

vividviolet: How are you doing?

mathletesmartin: Fine, I guess

vividviolet: That wasn't very convincing.

mathletesmartin: Is it that obvious?

vividviolet: Kinda, but I tend to pick up on those sorts of things. My mom says I'm a very empathetic person.

vividviolet: What's the matter?

mathletesmartin: Well...I don't know

mathletesmartin: It's kind of about my weird family stuff, and I don't want to make you deal with that.

vividviolet: Listen, if you're worried I'll judge you or tell people, don't be!

vividviolet: I've been on the receiving end of my fair share of judgment and gossip, even from my own family, like a few of my aunts and uncles. I would never ever ever *ever* do that to you.

mathletesmartin: I believe you, Vi, I just....

mathletesmartin: Um

mathletesmartin: So

mathletesmartin: I found this old video of my dad, before he left. And he basically said that he would hate to have a son like me.

vividviolet: Oh, Martin. I'm so sorry.

mathletesmartin: Thanks. I just don't know what to think or how to feel.

vividviolet: I think it's okay to feel however you feel.

vividviolet: But, Martin, you can't change who you are in your heart any more than I can change my legs. You didn't choose it, and it's not a bad thing either.

mathletesmartin: I guess

vividviolet: Look at me: my legs aren't a problem. Not to me, anyway. They're just a part of me, like my smile or my hair. Other people might see them as broken or shameful or something to wish away, but I don't. The way they feel about me is their problem, not mine.

mathletesmartin: That's true...but he's my *dad*. He's supposed to love me no matter what. If my own dad can't love who I am, how can anyone else?

vividviolet: You know that's not true, but I understand how you feel. Being adopted, it's hard, sometimes. I used to wonder why my birth parents didn't want me or what they'd think of me if they could see me now.

mathletesmartin: But you don't wonder about that stuff anymore?

vividviolet: Yes and no. I still wonder about that stuff. But now that I'm older, I try to remember that where a person comes from—their biological family, their DNA—is only a part of their story.

mathletesmartin: I guess so…

vividviolet: Take me, for example. My family has been going to the same synagogue since I was a baby, but we still get weird looks every once in a while. And now I'm getting ready for my bat mitzvah, right?

mathletesmartin: Sure

vividviolet: And all the kids in my preparation classes at the synagogue have known me *forever.* But the other day someone asked if it was harder for me to read Hebrew because it's "so different from Asian languages." I barely know any Vietnamese!

vividviolet: And look at you! Martin McLean? That sounds pretty Irish, but that's only a part of your background, right?

mathletesmartin: Yeah! I have family in Cuba and all over the place.

vividviolet: You see? You're so much more than the sum of your parts.

mathletesmartin: I know you're right. It just hurt so bad to hear him say those things.

vividviolet: I know. But Martin, from everything

I've heard about your dad, it sounds like he's never really been around. And that's *his* loss! Family is about being there for one another, regardless of DNA. Your family—your *real* family—is right here. And we're not going anywhere.

mathletesmartin: Thanks, Vi. You're really good at this. You should be a psychologist or something someday.

vividviolet: I'm actually planning on being a pediatrician. And maybe a composer, and a pastry chef too.

mathletesmartin: Wow! That's…a lot of jobs.

vividviolet: I have a lot of interests! But I like listening and helping people best of all. I'm sure you know that, well, that I get bullied a lot, for being in my chair and because I don't look like my mom and dad.

mathletesmartin: I'm sorry, Vi

vividviolet: Me too. I don't want to be anybody's inspirational poster, but I do want to put more good into the world than bad, you know?

mathletesmartin: Boy, you are *way* too good for Pickle.

vividviolet: Ha! I'm gonna tell him you said that.

☆ **10** ☆

Winter break came. We spent it in Chicago with Tío Billy and Uncle Isaiah at their new apartment near the lake, but I didn't feel much of the holiday spirit. I still couldn't get that video out of my head. It was like there was a version of myself in my mind, playing it over and over again, all the time. So I did what I'd always done—I clammed up. We saw all the lights on Michigan Avenue and went ice skating at Millennium Park, and I don't think I said more than ten words the whole time. I knew Mom noticed because I saw her exchanging glances with Tío Billy, but she didn't say anything about it either.

On Christmas Eve, Tío Billy beckoned me into the bathroom, where he and Uncle Isaiah had laid out all their makeup on the counter.

"Whoa," I said, surveying all the compacts and palettes and tubes.

"I know," Uncle Isaiah said, running a hand over his head sheepishly. "It looks like a Sephora exploded in here. But let it be known, this is *all* Billy's."

"Hardly!" Tío Billy laughed. "Okay, it's time for Makeup 101."

"Uh, Tío Billy?" I said. "I don't know if you noticed, but I'm not exactly my mother's son. There's no way I can do makeup."

"That's quitter talk!" Uncle Isaiah said, spritzing my face with something in a slim black bottle. I coughed. "Take a seat, sir. School is in session."

They worked as a team, wiping and slathering and dabbing all sorts of products over my face. As they added each new element, they talked me through what it was and how to use it. Primer, foundation, highlight, contour—it was like learning a new language.

"So for eyes, it's really 'go big or go home,'" Uncle Isaiah explained as Tío Billy swirled a little brush through a scarlet powder. "Though if you accidentally go *way* farther than you wanted to, you can clean up around the edges with some concealer."

"How did you learn all this?" I asked, closing one eye. Tío Billy swooped in and started swiping the shadow across my eyelid in short, light strokes.

Uncle Isaiah shrugged. "Drag makeup is a lot like stage makeup," he said, cleaning his hand with a makeup wipe. "When you do as much theater as we do, learning makeup is basically mandatory. Plus, *someone* had to help Billy beat his face when he was first starting out."

"Beat?" I exclaimed. *That sounds violent.*

Tío Billy laughed and pressed some loose glitter under my eyebrow where he had just applied a tacky primer.

"It just means doing your makeup," he said. "To be 'beat' means that you're painted for the gods, and to be 'painted for the gods' means—"

"That you're serving face?" I asked. Uncle Isaiah laughed in surprise, and Tío Billy looked impressed.

"Basically!" he said. "It all means that you're looking fierce."

It really is *another language,* I thought.

"You feeling good, Martin?" Uncle Isaiah asked. I cracked my unpainted eye and looked in the mirror. My other eye, done up in blazing reds, pinks, and gold, stared back at me.

"Wow," I said. "I don't even look like me."

"That's not true," Uncle Isaiah said, frowning a little. "You just look like a different version of you. A little more colorful, a little more pizazz."

"No, it's definitely a good thing," I said. "I look like Lottie."

"That's what we want to hear!" Tío Billy sang. He had me look down while he applied mascara, combing black goop onto my eyelashes to make them longer and darker. "Okay," he said, pulling away. "All done! Take a look."

"But you've only done half my face!" I protested, opening my eyes and staring at the bare side of my face in the mirror. Tío Billy laughed.

"That's because you're going to do the other half," he said. I blanched.

"Nuh-uh," I said, shaking my head. "It's going to look like a Picasso compared to your side."

"And Picasso's paintings are worth millions!" Uncle Isaiah said encouragingly, pushing the foundation and makeup sponge toward me. "Just try it. That's the only way any of us gets better."

One hour and many makeup wipes later, I had replicated their artistry on the other side of my face—sort of. I had drawn the crease of my eyeshadow too high, and my eyebrows, which Uncle Isaiah said were supposed to look like sisters, looked more like third cousins, twice removed. But overall, I was pleasantly surprised. I wasn't that bad!

"See?" Uncle Isaiah said. "A few more trial runs, and you'll be an old pro."

"Go ahead and take it off, león," Tío Billy said, handing me the pack of makeup wipes. "We've gotta get dinner started before your Mom chews her own arm off. You know how she gets when she's hangry!" He rolled his eyes and closed the door behind him and Uncle Isaiah.

Alone in the bathroom, I took a moment to really look at myself in the mirror. I wasn't fully Lottie, not yet, but I could see her in me, shimmering beneath the surface. My heart swelled with pride. *Painted for the gods,* I thought, smiling. I turned my face to admire my work from different angles. *Fierce.*

But then my thoughts flashed without warning to the video, to baby Martin in his heels and earrings, and to Dad's voice, echoing through my head.

You had better grow out of this . . .

I don't know how I could live . . .

He'd hate everything about Lottie. Which meant he'd hate everything about me.

And suddenly, I wasn't feeling very fierce at all.

★ ★ ★

The next morning, we opened presents beneath Tío Billy and Uncle Isaiah's tree. The whole apartment sparkled with Christmas lights and tea candles and the sun reflecting off the lake. I opened up a card from Mom first. Inside was a download code for a computer program.

"Ooh!" I plugged the name of the program into Google on my phone and read the description. It would allow me to look at constellations in the night sky anywhere in the world, and on any night in history. "This is amazing! It's like a time machine, but for astronomers!"

"I'm glad you like it, mijo," Mom said, and I leaned over to kiss her cheek.

Tío Billy slid a box toward me that was covered in tons of ribbons. Uncle Isaiah smiled at me from where he sat next to Mom on the couch.

"This is from your uncle Billy and me," he said. "We heard you were in need of something like this."

Something like this? I tore open the wrapping paper, tossing all the ribbons aside, and lifted the lid of the box. Gently peeling back the petals of tissue paper, I reached in and pulled out an unbelievably beautiful wig. It was like my natural hair, only bigger and better: a voluminous Afro with gorgeously defined curls the color of rich milk chocolate. My mouth fell open.

"It's perfect," I said, pulling it awkwardly onto my head. Over all my hair, it didn't sit right, and Tío Billy laughed.

"We got you a wig cap, too, león," he said, coming over to help me put it on properly. The wig had something called a lace front, which Tío Billy explained was a fancy kind of closure that made it look like the hair was really growing out of your head. You had to cover it with a little makeup, but Tío Billy promised that it would be easy enough for me to do on my own.

"It's too big!" Mom said, waving a Christmas cookie at me. "It's so 70s!"

"It's the trend right now. Everything old is new

again," Uncle Isaiah soothed. "It's real human hair, you know. That's the best kind of wig you can buy."

"Wow," I said, stroking the curls. "How do they get the hair?"

"People donate it or sell it," Uncle Isaiah explained. "There are women who intentionally grow their hair out real long and take extra-special care of it so they can cut it all off and have it made into wigs." He bounced a finger off the tip of my nose playfully. "Nothing but the best for Miss León!"

"Billy, where's my fancy wig? I could use a new 'do." Mom teased.

"You have waaaay too much hair for a wig, mamacita," Uncle Isaiah said, wiggling his fingers in Mom's direction. "You better work those natural curls, though." Mom fluffed her hair, looking pleased with herself.

"Does it look okay?" I asked anxiously. Everyone nodded enthusiastically.

"It's the perfect 'do for Lottie León," Tío Billy said. "Ferocious and fierce!" I giggled as he gave a lionlike growl.

"You're going to look perfect," Uncle Isaiah said. "Promise."

Later that night, as Mom packed our bags for the flight in the morning, I sat by the window and looked out at the lake. I held Lottie's new wig in my lap, letting the soft curls fall effortlessly through my fingers. As excited as I was about Lottie, I couldn't help thinking about Dad's video. And even though Violet had told me not to worry about what Dad would think, as I gazed at the wig, I kept hearing his voice. There had been hatred there, deep down beneath his joking tone, and I couldn't forget it.

I leaned my head against the cool window, wishing the thoughts out of my mind and the stinging tears out of my eyes. I heard the shuffle of fabric behind me and smelled Mom's jasmine perfume. She placed her hand on my shoulder.

"Mijo?" she asked. "What's wrong?"

"Nothing," I murmured, not looking at her. She sat down on the window seat across from me.

"You've been especially quiet this whole trip," she said. "Is something bothering you?"

"I don't want to talk about it," I said.

"Martín," she said, "you promised you'd talk to me."

"I don't want to!" I snapped. She looked surprised, and even I was startled by my sudden increase in volume.

"Hey," Mom scolded gently. "Don't raise your voice at me, Martín. I'm only asking because I'm worried about you."

"I—I know," I said, squeezing my eyes closed tight.

"So can you talk to me? Please?"

"It's just a lot," I said, wiping my nose with the

back of my hand. "School and Mathletes and drag . . ."

"I know," she said, scooping me up in her arms. "Baby, you don't have to do it all if you don't want to."

"I do!" I said. "I want to, a lot. But it's complicated, and it's all on the same night, and Nelson is a jerk, and Dad . . ." I trailed off. Mom rearranged herself so she could look me in the eye.

"Hey, what did you mean about your dad?" she asked, scanning my face for answers. "Did he reach out to you?" I shook my head.

"No," I said. "It was after I went up to the attic." And then I told her about the video. As I spoke, her face got very tight and very still. By the time I was done, I had stopped crying, but Mom looked like she was about to start.

"Mijo," she said quietly, "listen to me. Your dad, for all his imagination, could never have dreamed up a kid as amazing and incandescent as you."

"Incandescent?"

"It means 'burning brightly,'" she explained. "And that's what you do, Martin. You burn even brighter than those stars you love so much." She pressed her lips against my forehead and closed her eyes. "What your father would or wouldn't think of you doesn't matter, because he doesn't deserve you. So you can't worry about him, okay? Just worry about being yourself—your incredible, intelligent, fabulous self."

"Being myself is hard," I said. "Sometimes I don't know who that is."

"Por supuesto," Mom replied. "It can take your whole life to figure out who you are. You know, your abuela didn't want me to become an artist."

"She didn't?" Mom didn't talk about Abuelita Inez a lot. She died when I was pretty little, and she lived in Cuba, so I never really got to know her. From the bits and pieces I've been able to get out of Mom, I knew that she loved her kids, but she was pretty strict.

"No way! She wanted me to either get a job doing what she called 'real work,' like a doctor or a lawyer, or get married and have babies." She shrugged. "But I wanted to be a painter, so I got as many scholarships as I could and went to art school. And it was the best decision I ever made. Besides having you, of course."

"You met Dad at school, right?" I asked.

"When I went for my master's. He was a student in the film department. A real hot shot. He was going places." Mom's eyes drifted away from me, remembering. "If I hadn't followed my passion, you wouldn't be here. And your dad followed his passion, too, mijo. He just followed it away from us. Es triste, pero it is what it is."

"Yeah," I said, thinking. "Mom?"

"Yes, mijo?"

"I'm really sorry."

"For what, baby?" Mom wrinkled her brow.

"For yelling at you. I . . . I guess . . ." Mom opened her mouth to speak, but I kept going. "I guess I'm trying to follow my passion too. Like you and Dad. But the thing is, I don't want to be like Dad—I don't want to be mean to the people I love. And I haven't been doing a very good job of that. I've been trying to do so much at once, and it's been so hard, and sometimes I don't know how to talk about it. So I yelled. And I'm sorry. I'm really, really sorry."

"Oh, baby," she sighed. "I accept your apology." She put her hand under my chin. "But you could never, ever be like your dad. I promise. You're my sweet boy. And I love you, no matter what. You can grow up to be a drag superstar or a pet psychic or a synchronized swimmer, and I'll love you just the same!"

I smiled at that. I was so relieved she wasn't mad at me—I don't think my heart could have handled that.

"Did Abuelita Inez ever come around?" I asked.

"To me being an artist? I don't really know," Mom said. "She wished I were in a position to make more money, I know that. But I think she appreciated that I loved something enough to go out and get it, no matter what it took. And I'll never forget the look on her face when I gave her the first portrait I painted.

It was her in her rocking chair, by the fire at her house in Baracoa, smoking a cigarette." Mom smiled, but her eyes were teary. "She looked so proud, she was almost glowing. Like those old paintings of the saints." She leaned forward and held both my hands in hers.

"And that is how I feel about you, mijo," she said. "So, so proud. Please believe me: as long as you stay true to what's in here," and she tapped my chest, right over my heart, "you're going to be spectacular, baby."

Stay true to my heart? I thought. My heart felt so confused. What would staying true to it even look like? But then my eyes fell to my new wig, still splayed across my lap.

Lottie came straight from my heart, I realized. *She lived there for so many years without me even knowing.*

As Mom wrapped her arms around me and pulled me close, I hugged the wig against my chest. *And now that she's here, if I want to follow my heart . . . maybe first I have to follow Lottie's lead.*

JANUARY

PicknLittle: We have the perfect plan

LadyOfTheStage: We have the PERFECT plan!

PicknLittle: Ha, beat you to it

LadyOfTheStage: Rats!

mathletesmartin: A plan?

PicknLittle: Yes, a Patented Pickle Plan. Operation Calcu-Yaaas.

mathletesmartin: Um, what?

PicknLittle: I'm told "Yaaas!" is common parlance in the drag scene.

mathletesmartin: Told by who?!

PicknLittle: The YouTube.

LadyOfTheStage: And, of course, "calcu" as in "calculus."

PicknLitle: Calcu-yaaas.

mathletesmartin: I get it, I get it

LadyOfTheStage: Anyway, we've figured out how to get you to both the drag show AND Regionals all in one night.

PicknLitle: We're going to need some help, though. Like, an adult who's in on the plan.

LadyOfTheStage: Do you think your uncle would help?

mathletesmartin: I guess it depends on what you had in mind?

PicknLittle: Oh, we'd draw the line at murder

LadyOfTheStage: Pickle!

PicknLittle: Well, wouldn't we?

mathletesmartin: Oh, jeez

LadyOfTheStage: Listen, the night of the competitions, we'll have your Mathletes uniform in a go-bag and the car running.

mathletesmartin: Where did you get a car?!

LadyOfTheStage: Well, when I say we, I really mean your mom and uncle. It'll be one of their cars! Or, you know, a taxi. Ooh, or a limousine! I'm not picky.

PicknLittle: You're also not driving

LadyOfTheStage: A fair point

PicknLittle: Meanwhile, the three of us will get dropped off at Regionals.

mathlesemartin: Three of us?

vividviolet: Hi, guys!

LadyOfTheStage: Hi, Violet! Thanks for joining Operation Calcu-Yaaas.

vividviolet: I was super excited when Peter asked if I'd help plan. It's so *Game of Thrones*.

vividviolet: Only, you know, without all the murder and dragons.

LadyOfTheStage: Oh man, your mom lets you watch that?

vividviolet: She fast-forwards through the inappropriate stuff, but yeah.

PicknLittle: I mean, you don't *know* there won't be dragons...or murder.

LadyOfTheStage: Pickle! Stop that! Ugh, I'm so jealous, Vi.

mathletesmartin: Guys?

LadyOfTheStage: Sorry! Violet, we're just getting to your part.

vividviolet: Yes!

PicknLittle: So, right before the clock hits 7, I will suddenly make a Big Scene.

mathletesmartin: By doing...?

PicknLittle: ...Don't worry about it.

mathletesmartin: Pickle!

PicknLittle: What?!

LadyOfTheStage: I've already told him no fire.

vividviolet: And no fisticuffs.

LadyOfTheStage: Good rules to live by, really.

PicknLittle: Martin, relax. Of course there's a plan. Would I be Pickle "The Planner" Tufts otherwise?

LadyOfTheStage: I thought your middle name was "Silly Questions."

PicknLittle: Carmen!!! Not in front of Violet!!!

vividviolet: Aw, it's okay, Peter. Besides, technically *I* will be the one making a Big Scene.

LadyOfTheStage: Yesssssss. Enter Violet, stage left!

vividviolet: Obviously, we need a distraction beyond Peter...well, just being Peter. So I came up with an idea!

PicknLittle: It is, in fact, a pretty great idea. My

girlfriend is kiiind of a genius, you guys.

vividviolet: So here it is

vividviolet: Right before Regionals starts, I'm going to pretend to pass out. Just for a minute, but long enough for Peter to make the necessary Big Scene calling for help.

vividviolet: And, because they can't just ignore a medical emergency, they'll HAVE to delay the competition! For a little while, at least.

mathletesmartin: Violet, this is so nice, but you really don't have to do this if you're not comfortable with it.

vividviolet: Martin, I appreciate your concern, but this was my idea! Honestly, if a disabled person so much as sneezes, non-disabled people assume it's an emergency. It's pretty insulting. But, in this case, at least, I can use it to our advantage.

vividviolet: I wouldn't normally condone using one's disability to pull off a con, but . . . there's a championship and a queendom at stake, people!

LadyOfTheStage: Pickle, who knew you were dating a rebel?

PicknLittle: Isn't she the best?

vividviolet: Plus, I can make my sure my chair isn't in manual mode, so it'll be basically impossible for them to push me to the nurse's office. Sometimes being a wheelchair user has its perks!

LadyOfTheStage: Meanwhile, you'll be performing at Hoosier Mama

Just then, my phone vibrated with another ReadMe notification, which was extra weird considering I was already chatting with everyone I normally talked to. I quickly swiped to the home screen of the app, and my heart skipped a beat.

ReadMe App
JAN. 7—1:15 PM

This person would like to connect with you:
Christopher-Jack Cregg (NotJPTheOtherOne)
Message: Hey! It's Chris! Add me so we can chat!
mathletesmartin: Hey, Chris! Nice username.
NotJPTheOtherOne: Hey, thanks! Yours too!
mathletesmartin: What's up?
NotJPTheOtherOne: Nothing much. J.P.'s on the Xbox and Sara-Rose is watching some show on the PS4, so messing around on my phone was really the only option left for me.
mathletesmartin: Sara-Rose?
NotJPTheOtherOne: Oh, my little sister. She's in second grade. After her there's Mary-Anne and Grace-Elizabeth.
mathletesmartin: Wow, your parents really love hyphenated names, don't they?
NotJPTheOtherOne: To a fault. We're just lucky they didn't hyphenate their last names when they got married.

mathletesmartin: That bad?

NotJPTheOtherOne: Can you say Wojciechowski-Cregg?

mathletesmartin: I...cannot.

NotJPTheOtherOne: Exactly! So we count our blessings.

mathletesmartin: Seriously

mathletesmartin: Um, hey, could you give me one sec? I have to pop over to another chat really quick.

NotJPTheOtherOne: Sure thing!

As much as I wanted to stay and talk with Chris, plans were in motion in the other group chat. And it appeared that in my absence, all hell had broken loose.

ReadMe App
JAN. 7—1:23 PM

PicknLittle: All I'm saying is that if you needed a superhero to get the car to the competition without a driver, the Flash would be like, the WORST POSSIBLE CHOICE

LadyOfTheStage: Why?!

vividviolet: See, now you've got him started.

PicknLittle: All he can do is run fast!

LadyOfTheStage: Isn't that what we need?

Someone to run fast and push the car?

PicknLittle: HOW MUCH DO CARS WEIGH, CARMEN?

LadyOfTheStage: ...So?

vividviolet: Peter, play nice.

mathletesmartin: Uh, hi, guys, sorry. What's happening?

vividviolet: Oh, thank goodness you're back

PicknLittle: SUPERMAN IS THE OBVIOUS CHOICE, HE'S SO OVER-POWERED.

LadyOfTheStage: The conversation!!! Is over!!! Pickle!!!

PicknLittle: FINE

vividviolet: Basically, all you need to know is that right after your performance, you need to hop in the car and get to Baker's Lake Academy as fast as you can.

LadyOfTheStage: Google Maps says it's like a half-hour drive, but Pickle and Violet's distraction should delay the competition long enough for you to make it there in time. I'll be there, too, so I can stage-manage their performance. I am HIGHLY qualified, after all.

mathletesmartin: Should I warn Mr. Peterson that I'll be late?

PicknLittle: No way, dude. He'll just freak out.

LadyOfTheStage: You'll have to change in the car if you want to make it on time, though. Maybe throw some construction paper over the windows or something?

PicknLittle: Right, because with everything he'll have going on that night, strangers seeing his Snoopy underpants pass by at 60 miles per hour is DEFINITELY the biggest thing on his mind.

LadyOfTheStage: How do you know he's got Snoopy underpants?

PicknLittle: We've had sleepovers. Mind your business.

mathletesmartin: I hate you

PicknLittle: I kid, I kid! Anyway, by the time they're done making sure my Sleeping Beauty is a-okay, you should be rolling up to the school.

vividviolet: Leaving you plenty of time to wreck those Baker's Lake jerks!

LadyOfTheStage: Violet, the more I know about you, the more I like you.

PicknLittle: I know the feeling.

vividviolet: Aww!

LadyOfTheStage: Okay, now that's just gross.

I grinned to myself. It was all happening! My friends and I were all on good terms again, we had a plan for the big day, and Chris Cregg was talking to me. To *me*!

Is this real life? I thought, shaking my head in

disbelief. Then I remembered Chris was still waiting for me. *Shoot!*

mathletesmartin: Hey, sorry, I'm back! Anyway. Are you getting excited for Regionals?

NotJPTheOtherOne: Honestly, I'm way more excited about all things Mathletes since you've been captain.

NotJPTheOtherOne: Like, J.P.'s my brother and I love him, but he would have made a terrible leader. And Nelson is such a goon. You were the best choice.

mathletesmartin: Thanks, man. That means a lot.

NotJPTheOtherOne: Anyway, I'm mostly stoked to see the look on Mr. Berg's face when we crush his precious little team.

mathletesmartin: He'll probably just melt into the ground like the Wicked Witch of the West.

NotJPTheOtherOne: Ha! The Wicked Witch of Baker's Lake.

mathletesmartin: Exactly!

mathletesmartin: Hey, sooo I was wondering

NotJPTheOtherOne: What's up?

mathletesmartin: Do you want to come over?

mathletesmartin: We could practice for Mathletes

or we could play some video games like we talked about.

NotJPTheOtherOne: Like, right now?

mathletesmartin: Um, yeah, if that's okay?

NotJPTheOtherOne: That would be perfect! This house is so full of kids I can't even hear myself think. I can leave in like, 20 minutes?

mathletesmartin: Awesome. I'll send you my address!

I let out a strangled screech. The coolest guy in school—not to mention the nicest and the funniest and cutest—was coming over to hang out with me.

I could have dropped dead from excitement and absolute pants-wetting anxiety.

ReadMe App
JAN. 7—1:35 PM

mathletesmartin: Hey, guys? I've gotta run. But this plan sounds like it could actually work.

LadyOfTheStage: I told you it was perfect!

PicknLittle: Technically, *I* told him it was perfect first.

vividviolet: Hush, Peter.

LadyOfTheStage: Operation Calcu-Yaaas is a go!

vividviolet: Hear, hear!

mathletesmartin: Thanks, guys. And for moving a whole car, you'd want Hela from Thor. She can teleport stuff. Instant travel. Much better than Superman or The Flash. Bye!

PicknLittle: WHY THIS

☆ 11 ☆

Chris. Cregg. Was. Coming. Over.

And my room is a garbage pit! It was a five-alarm, code red, call-the-fire-department, call-the-Coast-Guard emergency. It'd been forever since I'd had someone over who wasn't Pickle or Carmen, and they were used to my mess. Chris couldn't see my old Lincoln Logs and stuffed animals.

As I whirled around in a tornado of tidying, the butterflies in my stomach returned, fluttery and vaguely nauseating. *I hope he still likes me after actually spending time with me.* Chris and I saw each other at Mathletes all the time, but there was a big difference between school friends and friend-friends. I wanted Chris to be a friend-friend, like Pickle and Carmen.

By the time the doorbell rang, my bedroom floor was mostly visible, and all my dirty laundry had been shoved under the bed. *Good enough*! I ran downstairs and prayed he wouldn't notice I was a little out of breath.

I opened the door to find Chris on the front stoop, wearing an army-green coat and matching scarf.

"Hey!" he said. "Nice place. I like this side of town. Lots of trees." He shifted his skateboard under his arm and smiled. "I skated over. No snow after New Year's meant I could bust out the board early!"

Immediately upon seeing the living room, Chris's eyes grew wide. Mom's bright mural with all the flowers and vines and—oh no—*my* face, had captured his attention. *How,* how *did I forget about the mural?* My face, the one actually attached to me, went hot.

"Whoa," Chris said, kicking off his shoes. He walked farther into the room, his mouth hanging open. "Your mom did all this?"

I nodded. "She's an artist. She teaches at the university too. Color Theory in Painting, with Professor Perez. But this is what she does in her spare time. She's out back in her studio right now."

"Wow. It's really good!" Chris tilted his freckled face up toward the ceiling as he unbuckled his helmet, taking in Mom's clouds and birds. "Is your dad an artist too?"

"Um, no. My dad's not around anymore," I said.

Chris opened his mouth, probably to apologize, but I rushed to talk over him. "He's a filmmaker though, which I guess is sort of like an artist. He's in Los Angeles."

"Oh," Chris nodded, looking relieved. "That's cool. Has he made anything I would've seen?" I shook my head.

"I think he mostly does, like, weird indie stuff. I don't really know."

"You've never seen one of his movies?"

"Nope," I said. Then, quickly changing the subject: "You wanna see my room?"

Upstairs, I showed Chris my video game collection and my superhero posters and the shelf where I keep all our Mathletes trophies. We decided on Minecraft and plopped down into the bean bag chairs near my TV as the Xbox started up. I handed Chris a controller in silence. *Say something, Martin!* I urged myself.

"Your hands are really dry," I said, without thinking. *Oh, God. Something* other *than that.* Chris looked down at his hands, surprised, and laughed.

"I know," he said. "It's from pottery. When you throw pots you get a lot of stuff on your hands, and then you have to wash it off. All that washing and soap can make your hands look like crocodile feet." He made his hand look like a crocodile mouth and chomped up and down.

"My mom's hands look like that too," I said, "from painting."

"I bet!" he said. "She does some cool stuff. Maybe she and I could talk about it some time."

"She'd like that," I said. But really, I was thinking about how that implied Chris wanted to hang out with me again. As the game booted up, Chris looked around my room.

"Cool stars," he said, pointing to my ceiling. "Did you do the constellations with them?"

"Nah," I said, "I made up my own."

"Your own constellations?"

I nodded.

"Do they have names?"

"Um, yeah," I said, "but only for me. I've never, like, written them down or anything."

"Show me one!" he said, pointing to the ceiling-sky. "Like that one, with the swoop and the part that looks like a sword. Is that Martinius, The Warrior?" I laughed and shook my head.

"Nope. That's Ferrum Masculinitum."

"Ferruh-what?"

"Ferrum, the Latin word for iron, and masculinitum—"

"—meaning man, right? Iron Man!" Chris exclaimed. "You named a constellation after Iron Man? In Latin?"

I shrugged. "It's closer to Pig Latin than the real thing. I make up a lot of my own words."

"What about that one?" Chris said, pointing to a swirly one in the center of the ceiling.

"That one's called Gena Major," I said, "for my mom."

"And that one?"

"Kevinax."

"Who's Kevin?"

"Um, my dad," I said. "Hey, the game's ready to go."

There was a pause before Chris picked up his controller from his lap. I tried not to look over, because I knew I'd see him looking back at me with pity.

"I'm sorry about your dad," he said. "I didn't know."

"You couldn't have," I said softly.

"Um, are we okay?"

"Yeah, of course. I'm not gonna get mad at you over my silly dad stuff."

"It's not silly," Chris said, looking very serious. "It must really suck." The genuine sympathy in his blue eyes caught me off guard. Startled by the butterflies zooming around in my stomach again, I blinked hard and looked away.

"Sometimes," I said. "But other times it doesn't feel like anything, because we've gotten so used to him being gone."

"Do you like having your uncle here?"

"Uh-huh," I nodded, my eyes fixed on the TV screen. "My uncle Billy is awesome. He has to move to Chicago soon, but he promised to . . ." I realized I couldn't tell Chris what Tío Billy promised—to stick around for All-Ages night—so I coughed and quickly came up with something else. "He promised to come visit when he can."

"Well, maybe when he's gone, we could hang out," Chris said. "That way you won't feel lonely or anything."

"That's . . . really nice of you. Thanks," I said, blushing a little. "And, I mean, I bet you wouldn't mind getting out of your house every once in a while, with all those siblings."

Chris laughed, and it was like a crack of lightning, but lovely.

"You have *no* idea," he said. "It's a zoo."

And then something happened. I was looking at Chris, who was so focused on the game, and all I wanted to do was tell him about Lottie. *Maybe he would understand, like Carmen and Pickle did,* I thought, feeling the words rise up in my throat. *Maybe he would think it's cool. Maybe he'd even want to see me perform.* I imagined Chris's face in the audience at Hoosier Mama, beaming with pride at watching me, and it was like the butterflies in my stomach were rushing around on a sugar high. My whole body felt as luminous as stardust, glowy and warm and hopeful. *Is this a crush?* I wondered. *Is this like-liking someone?*

I pushed all the thoughts aside. *Don't make it awkward, Martin. Just enjoy hanging out with him. Focus on the game.* So I did, and together Chris and I built a barn and a moat, and fought off hordes. While we played, we talked about all sorts of things—comics and Mathletes and whether or not Poppy would say yes when Nelson inevitably asked her to the spring formal. (I said no way, Chris said yes.)

"So what does your uncle do?" Chris asked. All of a sudden, I was hyperaware of my hands starting to sweat over my controller.

"He works in theater," I said, trying to sound casual.

"Oh, cool, like an actor?"

Say it, I thought. *You can tell him. Tell him that Tío Billy is a drag queen. Tell him about Lottie.*

"Not exactly," I said. "He runs a theater company with his husband." And then I paused, expecting him to laugh at the word "husband," to make the jokes that all the other seventh-grade boys would.

But Chris just nodded his head thoughtfully. "That's cool," he said. I swallowed. *Now's your chance!*

"But he also does some onstage stuff too," I said. His phone buzzed in his pocket, so he put down his controller to grab it. "Like sometimes he performs, um, in drag."

I waited with my heart in my throat, barely able to force my eyes away from the TV screen. When I finally did, Chris had gone pale—really pale. He leapt out of the beanbag chair, startling me.

"Chris?" I said, though it came out strangled. "What's wrong?" My mind had already taken off racing. *Maybe I had gone too far, bringing up Tío Billy like that. Maybe Chris wasn't as cool as I thought.*

"Oh, man," he said, without looking up from his phone. "I'm really sorry. I have to go."

"What is it? What's wrong?" I asked again, feeling the panic grip me. Was it mentioning drag? Did that scare him? Did he think I was gay? And did he hate me for it?

"Oh, man, I am in so much trouble," Chris said. "Uh . . . shoot . . . I left my siblings alone for two seconds and now—shoot, I'm so sorry, Martin. I'll explain later. I really have to go."

He can't even look me in the eye. My mind swirled like a hurricane. *And now he's come up with a story to bail himself out. So he doesn't have to hang out with someone like me.* Chris had already made his way downstairs, and when I finally got to the landing, he was pulling on his shoes. He grabbed his skateboard and turned his flushed face toward me.

"I'll, uh, talk to you later," he said, looking completely freaked. "Seriously, Martin, I'm so sorry! I'll text you!" He waved goodbye, but he was already mostly out the door. It closed behind him with a dull thud.

My chest tightened like a vice around my lungs. *Everything's falling apart.* Hot, stinging tears blurred my vision as I sat down on the stairs. *Everything's spinning out of control, and I can't stop it. I can't be Martin and Lottie at the same time. I can barely handle being just Martin.* I tried to breathe in, but it became a shuddering sob. *And if this is how Chris reacted to Tío Billy and drag, how could I ever tell him—or anyone—about Lottie? My dad and now Chris—who else is going to ditch me the second they realize who I really am?*

I shouldn't have said anything at all.

I shouldn't have said anything at all.

I shouldn't ever *say* anything *at all.*

"León!"

Tío Billy's voice broke through my panic. I hadn't realized he was home, but suddenly he was rushing over to me.

"What's wrong? Did you hurt yourself? Hey, hey, look at me." I tried to meet his eyes with mine. "Deep breaths, okay? Match my breathing. In and out, león, nice and steady."

"I told Chris Cregg you're a drag queen!" I blurted out. "I told him and he left and now he hates me, I'm sure of it!" Then I spilled my guts, telling Tío Billy everything—Chris coming over, and how nice he was, and the butterflies and the video games, and how I was sure he left because he hated drag queens and anyone who associated with them. When I was done, Tío Billy put his arm around me and sighed.

"Oh, león," he sighed. "Why would he hate you for that, huh?"

"Because now he'll think I'm weird," I sniffled. "I should have kept my mouth shut."

"Hey," Tío Billy said calmly, stroking my hair. "I don't ever want you talking like that. It is always right to speak your truth, you hear me? And as for this Chris . . ." He made a point to look me right in the eyes, and he spoke very slowly. "Just because something's different doesn't mean it's something to hate. And if this boy is so quick to hate you, then let him."

"What?" *Let him hate me?*

"You heard me. Let him. Because if he's the type of person who would hate somebody for how they dress, or what they like, then he's not the type of person you want in your life."

"He's really cool," I sniffled. "And nice. And he likes comics."

"If you've judged him to be of good character, then maybe it's not what you think," Tío Billy replied. "Maybe he was so thrilled to find a friend with such amazing interests that he had to run home right away to write it all down in his diary with sparkly gel pens!"

I giggled, though I didn't feel like it. Tío Billy gave me a kind smile.

"All I'm saying is that the only people who deserve space in your life are the people who appreciate everything you are. And you are talented and fierce and brave," he said. "So who cares if this kid freaked out? The show must go on. And your life, león, is one fabulous show. Don't miss out on it."

I knew Tío Billy was right, but I still felt a little sick and a little sad.

"Can we practice my routine some more?" I asked, wiping my nose.

"Would that make you feel better?" he asked.

I nodded. "I think so," I said.

Tío Billy smiled a little and clapped me on the shoulder. "Then put your heels on, girl. We've got work to do."

★ ★ ★

Later that night, as I was winding down for bed, I heard my phone vibrate. When I saw that Chris wanted to chat, I felt sick to my stomach. *What if he flips out at me for being a freak?* I wondered, my hands shaky as I swiped into my phone. *What if he's just like Nelson, after all?* Swallowing my nerves, I opened the chat.

★ ★ ★

NotJPTheOtherOne: Hey!

mathletesmartin: Hi

NotJPTheOtherOne: I am so, so sorry for bailing on you today.

mathletesmartin: It's okay. You were surprised.

NotJPTheOtherOne: You have no idea. I can't believe my sister ended up in the hospital.

mathletesmartin: Wait, what?!

mathletesmartin: The hospital?

NotJPTheOtherOne: Oh, man, I guess I didn't really explain

NotJPTheOtherOne: Soooo, yeah. I was supposed to be watching the girls, but...

NotJPTheOtherOne: Well, I really wanted to hang out with you! and J.P. was there, so I thought it would be okay.

mathletesmartin: And it wasn't?

NotJPTheOtherOne: I guess I was gone just long enough for Grace-Elizabeth to jump off the couch and break her arm.

mathletesmartin: Whoa! Is she okay?

NotJPTheOtherOne: See for yourself

CHRISTOPHER-JACK CREGG (NotJPTheOtherOne) has added an image to the chat: IMG01071801.jpg

mathletesmartin: Oh man, that looks bad

NotJPTheOtherOne: Yeah, apparently it was pretty gruesome. Sara-Rose yelled for J.P., and he got our neighbor to drive them to the emergency room. My mom met them at the hospital, but she was really mad.

mathletesmartin: I bet

NotJPTheOtherOne: Anyway, I just wanted to say sorry for ditching you like that. It was my bad for leaving my siblings with J.P. in the first place. I didn't mean to be a jerk.

mathletesmartin: You weren't! I mean, it's fine! I'm glad your sister is okay.

NotJPTheOtherOne: Maybe we can hang out again soon?

NotJPTheOtherOne: Outside of school, I mean

NotJPTheOtherOne: And preferably when I'm not supposed to be babysitting . . .

mathletesmartin: Yeah, that'd be great!

NotJPTheOtherOne: I know Mathletes is heating up, but it would be cool to have a break from all that, you know?

NotJPTheOtherOne: Though I bet you're looking forward to Regionals more than anybody

mathletesmartin: I guess so

NotJPTheOtherOne: What's wrong?

mathletesmartin: What do you mean?

NotJPTheOtherOne: You just don't seem very excited. Regionals was all you could talk about last year!

mathletesmartin: It's just kind of complicated for

me this year, is all.

NotJPTheOtherOne: Oh. Well, you don't have to talk about it if you don't want to.

mathletesmartin: No, it's not like that...I'm worried because I'm not sure I'll make it to Regionals this year.

NotJPTheOtherOne: WHAT?!

mathletesmartin: Yeah, I've sort of got a conflict.

mathletesmartin: A...personal thing.

mathletesmartin: I have a plan and everything, but there's still a chance I won't make it to Baker's Lake in time.

NotJPTheOtherOne: But we have to have you there!

mathletesmartin: You don't, though! You're all so good.

NotJPTheOtherOne: No way! You're the captain! We need you!

mathletesmartin: I don't know. It might not happen. I want to be there super bad! But...

NotJPTheOtherOne: Oh man. Martin, I don't know what's going on that would keep you from Regionals, and I guess I don't really need to know, but seriously. We can't do this without you.

NotJPTheOtherOne: You've kept us together all year!

NotJPTheOtherOne: And we've never been better, or quicker.

NotJPTheOtherOne: The team just wouldn't be

the same without you.

mathletesmartin: That's really nice, but you can win without me.

NotJPTheOtherOne: But I don't want to.

mathletesmartin: Oh

NotJPTheOtherOne: Yeah! So you have to make it.

mathletesmartin: I'll try, really hard.

NotJPTheOtherOne: Promise?

mathletesmartin: I promise.

Chris and I chatted a little more before we both logged off, but I don't think I processed a word. He didn't have anything against drag queens at all I—had just convinced myself he did. My secret was safe, and I couldn't stop thinking about him saying he didn't want to win without me. I felt like the wings of all those butterflies in my stomach were lifting me up, up, and far away.

Maybe it was the butterfly wings that carried me over to my closet. I opened the doors to look at Lottie's outfit. I reached out and touched the beautiful dress, the beads glittering beneath my fingertips, and the jacket covered in jewels so bright they reminded me of candy. I took them out and laid them on my bed, then found my shoes and my wig and the makeup Mom lent me. Carefully, I undressed and slipped the heavy gown over my head, struggling to zip up the back. The jacket hung off my slender shoulders, effortlessly chic. I sat on my bed and used the mirror inside a blush compact to stumble through the makeup routine Tío Billy and Uncle Isaiah had taught me, paying extra attention to my eyes. I drew myself a big red mouth to finish, smacking my lips together in the mirror like I'd seen Mom do a million times.

When my makeup was finished and I had situated my wig over the wig cap as best I could, I realized this was the first time I would see myself in full drag. I took a deep breath and hopped off my bed, standing with my back to the long hanging mirror mounted on my bedroom door. *When you turn around, you're going to see Lottie León, not Martin McLean. This is it.*

Slowly, I turned. When I opened my eyes, my stomach dropped to my toes. I didn't recognize the person in front of me. She was tall and leggy, with deep set eyes and full lips and a beauty mark on her cheek.

When I moved my arm, so did Lottie. When I smiled, wide and uncontrollable, so did she. The person in the mirror sparkled. Her posture was perfect and her hands were graceful. She looked totally at ease. She was beautiful. She was confident.

And she was me.

★ ★ ★

LadyOfTheStage: Good morning, beautiful!

mathletesmartin: Yeeeees?

LadyOfTheStage: Today's the day! The sun is shining! The birds are singing!

PicknLittle: The drag queens are primping!

LadyOfTheStage: Pickle!

mathletesmartin: Well, he's not wrong

vividviolet: Ooh, you're already getting ready? I want to see! Send pictures!

mathletesmartin: No way! I haven't even left yet.

PicknLittle: Yeah, a lady never sends selfies too early, or too late. She sends selfies precisely when she means to.

LadyOfTheStage: Kim Kardashian?

PicknLittle: A paraphrased Gandalf the Grey.

LadyOfTheStage: Of course

vividviolet: Fiiiiine. Martin, you should rest easy knowing everything re: Operation Calcu-Yaaas is under control!

PicknLittle: We're very well prepared.

LadyOfTheStage: I'm so excited for you! You're going to kick butt.

LadyOfTheStage: Or, Lottie's going to kick butt

LadyOfTheStage: You both are

LadyOfTheStage: Jeez, what's the appropriate way to say that?

mathletesmartin: Um, either. I guess I'm me when I'm offstage, but I'm Lottie when I'm onstage. Does that make sense?

vividviolet: Ugh, I so wish we could be there! Take SO many pictures.

LadyOfTheStage: Oh, drat, I have to go. Gotta take Woofecito out. I forgot to earlier and now he's doing a tap dance by the door.

PicknLittle: Tap dance, you say? Sounds like a talented pup. Maybe he wants to sign up for a certain All-Ages Night, give Martin a little run for his money?

LadyOfTheStage: Hardee-har

mathletesmartin: Don't joke. Woofecito could easily take me down.

vividviolet: All right, all right, let's leave Martin alone to get ready. Beauty takes time!

PicknLittle: Not for you.

LadyOfTheStage: GAG ME. (I still love you, Vi.)

vividviolet: (Love you too!)

mathletesmartin: And on that note...

☆ 12 ☆

I spent the morning of the competitions trying to keep my breakfast down. I was nauseated and shaking and felt like I might vibrate right out of my body. Mom told me to stop pacing the living room, but I couldn't help it. I knew if I could just get to the show, I could make it through the rest of the day somehow.

Tío Billy told me it was customary for the queens to get ready at "the gig," so at 3:30 (finally!) we piled into the car with all of Lottie's clothes and makeup stuffed into shopping bags. I packed my Mathletes uniform in my backpack and stashed it in the passenger seat.

When we pulled up to Hoosier Mama, the old Victorian house seemed to loom over me, as if, at any moment, it would bend down and ask what I thought I was doing there.

"Hey, it's Lottie León, queen of the jungle!"

Dorie appeared as I hopped out of the car, swooping me up into one of her big hugs. Dorie reminded me of a kindly lady hobbit, because she always smelled like warm bread with butter, or caramel rolls, or other yummy things.

"Dorie, lions live in the savannah," I said as we pulled apart.

"I know, I know. But 'jungle' sounds so much cooler, am I right?" She laughed and turned her attention to Mom. "Gena, yeah? I'm Dorie."

"Yes, hi," Mom said, lowering one of our bags to the ground, "Billy has told me so much about you!"

"I could say the same," Dorie said, shaking her hand. "And I have to tell you, you're just as beautiful as he described." Mom blushed the color of apricots. *I can't even remember the last time I saw Mom blush.*

"Thank you!" Mom said, smiling wide. "You are too sweet! Martin, we better get you inside."

"Of course," Dorie said. "Let me show you where the staging area is."

We lugged all our bags behind us as we followed Dorie through the accessible side entrance and took the elevator downstairs to a room behind the stage.

"This is the green room," Dorie said cheerfully. Then she leaned in close to me and whispered, "It's not actually green. Don't tell!"

She swung open the door, and Mom started

coughing because the air was so thick with hairspray. I looked around and counted six queens already seated at stations along a mirrored wall, with only a few empty spaces remaining.

"You can set up here," Dorie said, gesturing to a space between two performers who were already well into their makeup routines. "And just holler if you need anything!" She kissed Tío Billy on the cheek and disappeared.

Mom leapt into action, unpacking my wig and setting it up on a Styrofoam head she got at the beauty supply store. Tío Billy gestured to the chair.

"Okay, león," he said as I took a seat. He knelt to my level and lowered his voice, as though we were discussing strategy for a high-stakes mission. And I guess in a way, we were. "You want me to do your makeup, or can you handle it?"

"Um, could you do it?" I asked, looking around the room at the other queens. "I just want to look perfect, and . . ." I held up my hands for him to see. They were shaking like maracas.

"Of course," he said, without skipping a beat. "Let's get to it."

As he helped me wrangle on a wig cap, I watched the queens next to me in the mirror. To my left, a teenager, maybe eighteen, was carefully swiping on a glittery green eyeshadow with the side of his pinky finger. He had gorgeous, sculpted cheekbones and a stuck-up look about him, as though he were on his way to tea with the Queen of England or something. His eyes shifted to the side, catching me staring. I jumped in my seat. He glared, so I quickly swiveled my gaze to my right, where a heavyset man in his mid-thirties (I think?) was doing something weird to his eyebrows.

The man was combing his eyebrows upward with a little brush and slathering Elmer's Glue over them straight from the twist-up stick, like his face was an arts and crafts project. Then he layered on an orange-colored concealer, plus foundation and powder, over the area he had just glued down. In a matter of minutes, it was as though he had never had eyebrows at all.

"Kind of like magic, huh?" he said to me when he was finished. I blinked, surprised he'd even address me, and then I realized who he was: *Aida Lott!* The beautiful queen I had seen at my first show! My face turned hot.

"It—it is," I stuttered, starstruck. "Is it hard to wash off?"

"You know, I'm in drag so much these days, sometimes it feels like I should just shave the damn things off."

"People do that?" I asked. Tío Billy nodded and set to work applying foundation to my face with an egg-shaped pink sponge.

"Oh, yeah," Aida said, taking a dark cosmetics pencil to an area well above her natural brow. "People do all sorts of weird things to look good in drag. And just when I feel like I've seen it all, some new trend comes out and blows me away." Aida and Tío Billy exchanged a knowing look.

"How long have you been doing drag?" I asked. Immediately I worried that I had asked a rude question. But Aida answered right away.

"Oh, wow, fifteen years? Give or take?"

"And you're still an amateur?"

She burst out laughing. *Okay,* that *was definitely a rude question.* The blood rushed to my face. "I just mean—All-Ages Night is for amateurs and I—um—" I stammered, but she didn't seem to be offended.

"Oh, honey," she fanned her face with her hands to keep the tears of laughter from ruining her makeup. "I haven't been read like that in a minute." Behind me, Tío Billy shook with silent laughter too. "Yes, handsome, I'm still an amateur. Haven't managed to hit it big yet, plus, momma's gotta pay her bills. I'm an anesthesiologist when I'm not performing."

Fifteen years! And still an amateur! Clearly, I had a lot to learn, and a *long* way to go. I swept the room with my eyes and wondered how many of the other performers had been doing drag for that long.

Aida gestured to me with her pencil, raising an eyebrow. "You know, I was just about your age when I started messing around with drag."

"Really?" I asked. Tío Billy swiped a warm brown contour shade into the hollows of my cheeks.

"Sure. Oh, I wasn't competing or anything like that, just flouncing around in dresses and makeup in my bedroom. You're lucky—there was no way I could have been performing when I was as young as you." She started to work on her other eyebrow, sketching in an arching shape with light, feathery strokes. "No, the world has changed since I was a kiddo. Now there's all sorts of ways for young people to get involved in the scene. You're living in the golden age of drag, my friend."

She stuck out her hand, like an old-timey princess with her wrist sort of limp as though she expected it to be kissed.

"I'm Aida Lott," she said.

"I know," I said bashfully. Then I realized she was waiting for me to introduce myself too. "I'm . . . Lottie León."

The name felt so right coming off my lips and in my voice. I took her hand, and we didn't shake, just sort of squeezed each other's palms respectfully. It was like a meeting of two powerful ambassadors, and it made me feel very professional, like a real drag queen.

"It's very nice to meet you, Miss Lottie," Aida said. "Break a leg tonight."

"That means 'good luck,'" Tío Billy whispered in my ear.

"I know!" I hissed back. But I couldn't help smiling. *I've made my first drag queen friend. So far, so good.*

Tío Billy worked on my face, carefully applying hot pink glitter and big false lashes, and the room began to fill up. More queens and their entourages arrived with makeup cases and wig stands in tow, loudly claiming the empty spots at the mirror. The fuller the room became, the more Mom started to pace.

"Why don't you go save us some seats, Gena?" Tío Billy asked, as Mom wrung her hands for the millionth time. She looked relieved to be dismissed.

"Okay," she said, putting an arm around me. "I'll be rooting for you out there, baby."

"Big crowds make your mother nervous," Tío Billy said after Mom left the room. He added the finishing touches to my lipstick with a flourish. "Speaking of mothers," he said as he sharpened his brown eye pencil. "Have you ever heard of drag families?" I shook my head.

"In drag culture, more experienced queens tend to sort of 'adopt' new ones. They become drag mother and daughter." He blew a flurry of pencil shavings off the liner with a flourish. "I know Lottie León and Cassie Blanca don't share a name, but I think it's fair to say they're family, don't you?"

"Definitely."

"Would you like me to be your drag mother?" Tío Billy asked gently.

"Of course!" I exclaimed. *I have a drag mother*!

"Ah-ah-ah! Don't move!" Tío Billy had me relax my face, then he penciled in a beauty mark just like the one Cassie Blanca had, on my left side. "There. Perfect! Okay, wig time."

★ ★ ★

Shortly before the show was set to start, Dorie poked her head into the green room.

"Listen up, ladies!" she called over the din of house music and excited chatter. She lifted a sheet of paper above her head. "I have in my hand the walking order for the preliminary round!"

An icy bolt of confusion shot through me. *Walking order? Preliminary round?*

"I'm posting it here," Dorie gestured behind her to the door. "Take a look and then line up backstage in order, please. You're on in ten."

"Thank you, ten!" A few voices called from behind me, but I barely heard them. I spun around to face Tío Billy, who had gone white.

"Preliminary round?" I asked, my voice rising. "What preliminary round?" Tío Billy muttered a stream of curse words in Spanish.

"I didn't know, león, I swear," he said. "Dorie never said anything about a prelim."

"What am I supposed to do?" I wailed. "I only prepared one routine! And I'll never make it to Regionals in time if I have to do two rounds!"

"Okay, okay, don't panic," Tío Billy said. "Give me a minute." And he darted out the door after Dorie.

I stood in the center of the room, feeling helpless with my sweaty palms and shaky legs. After a minute or two, Tío Billy returned. Queens were already beginning to file out the door, getting in order backstage.

"So," he began, "here's the deal. It's a walk-off. The walk-off round determines who goes on to compete in the routine portion."

"A walk-off?" I cried. "I don't know how to do a walk-off! I didn't practice for a walk-off!"

"Yes, you did!" Tío Billy said. "All you have to do is walk down to the front of the stage and back, giving all that Lottie León attitude. That's it!"

"I don't know . . ."

"You can do it, león. I know it. And you go on fourth, which is good! Not too early in the show, not too late. The crowd will remember you that way. You're after Anita Paycheck."

"Who's she?" I asked. Tío Billy pointed discreetly to the teenager who had glared at me earlier. Now, as Anita, she was wearing a long auburn wig and barely any clothes at all, just a sparkly baby-pink bikini.

"Oh, no," I said, going pale. "She seemed kind of mean."

"Don't worry about her," Tío Billy said firmly. "Focus on you. Pretend you're walking in the living room at home. Just be waiting on the stage right side when Anita goes on, okay? When she gets offstage, Dorie will announce you, then you just do your thing."

"But what about the second round?" I asked.

"Let me worry about that right now," he said firmly. "Just give this walk everything you've got, and we'll figure out the rest once we get you to Regionals."

"Okay. Okay, okay, okay, I can do this. I can do this," I repeated. *Maybe if I say it enough times, it will become true.* But true or not, I had come too far to give up on Lottie now—this walk-off was happening. I looked down at my glittery heels, then at Tío Billy. "Thank you," I said. "For helping me get here. For everything."

"No way. I should be thanking you, león," he said. "Cassie Blanca might have been your inspiration, but Lottie León? She's mine."

I felt that telltale lump in my throat, but Tío Billy distracted me by throwing our special handshake—followed by a big bear hug. I breathed in deep the scent of his cologne and tried to steady myself.

"Now go bring Lottie to the people!" he whispered. With one final adjustment to my wig, he turned and left me in the green room, alone.

Gulp.

I can do this. Can I do this? Why did I think I could do this? I was so nervous, I was trembling like Woofecito in the snow. *What if I shake right out of my shoes?*

Don't think about failing, I urged myself as I made my way backstage. Nearly all the queens had lined up backstage. It was almost time. *What would Lottie do? She'd stomp the runway, that's what. So that's what she's* going *to do.*

The house lights dimmed out in the audience as I found my place among the other queens. I could see strobes and flashing colors from where I stood in the wings, concealed by the curtain. In front of me, Anita Paycheck adjusted her bikini bottom. Dorie's voice blared out from over the speakers.

"All right, all right! Let's get it started! Bargain Basement Babes at Hoosier Mama is bringing you the best in amateur entertainment this evening: it's All-Ages Night!" The crowd whooped and hollered, and I heard Tío Billy's two-finger whistle from the stage right side. "This competition is open to queens of any age, so get ready to see some new talent—and some damn near ancient ones too." The crowd laughed, and I could hear Dorie's grin as she continued.

"Tonight, our queens are being judged by the audience. That means whoever gets the most applause and the best audience reaction is the winner of fame, fortune, and our fabulous prize of one thousand dollars! So, are you ready to show these ladies some love?" The crowd stomped and cheered. I was smiling—*When did that happen?*— but I felt like my heart might beat out of my chest. *I want to win so badly. I have to.* Not just to prove my worth to the other queens or to win money for a new telescope—I wanted to win for me.

"Okay, then! Let's get this prelim round started! Give a hearty Hoosier Mama welcome to our first queen, Aida Lott!"

The lights dimmed again, and the music started up with a song I recognized right away from Tío Billy's pump-up playlist: "Sissy That Walk." *RuPaul!* I thought with some relief. *I know her, I love her. At least that might work in my favor.*

Upon hearing the music, Aida stepped out on stage. She wore a perfectly coiffed blonde wig and, with all her makeup and huge lashes, looked just like a Barbie doll. She wore a cherry red dress made of some kind of shiny material, and the tallest black stilettos I had ever seen.

Aida looked amazing out there on the stage, strutting her stuff, but I was too anxious to enjoy her walk. And it was over in a flash; I blinked, and she was already headed offstage—to thunderous applause, of course. *Could I ever be half that good?* I thought, clapping with sweaty hands. Aida came into the wings and winked at me as she passed by.

"You did great!" I whispered, as Dorie called out the next performer's name.

"Thank you, sweetheart!" Aida whispered back. She leaned down and gave me an air kiss, right next to my ear, so she wouldn't mess up my makeup. "You're going to kill it."

I didn't even remember the next queen, I was so wrapped up in my nerves. *All you have to do is walk. That's it! Just walk. You've been doing it forever. Sure, the heels are new, but you've practiced. You're good. You're fine.* But when I closed my eyes, I saw flashes of memory:

Falling on my face in my tutu trying to reach Carmen.

Running out of Mr. Peterson's class, my chest tight.

My little feet in a pair of big pumps, toddling over to Dad and his video camera—and tumbling over.

"You can bet your bottom dollar she'll give you a good show. She is . . . Anita Paycheck!"

Oh my God. I'm next. Anita cartwheeled onto the stage from the wings, her foot nearly colliding with my chin as she launched herself forward. I yelped and jumped back as Aida Lott sidled up next to me.

"That girl always does the absolute most," she said, rolling her eyes. A wave of cheers and applause rose as Anita sashayed down to the edge of the stage. Aida squeezed my shoulder. "Go get 'em, sweets."

This was it. The moment I'd been waiting for. Martin McLean as Lottie León, live on stage. For the first time in my life, all eyes would be on me. No hiding, no fading into the background, no staying silent. *If it all crashes and burns . . .*

I closed my eyes and smiled to myself. If it was all going to crash and burn, then at least, for one night, I was brave.

As Anita began to flip-flop offstage, I heard the words I had been waiting months for the world to hear: "Next up, it's . . . Lottie León!"

This is it, I thought. *This could be your only chance to impress everyone. Go!*

I was so focused on getting onstage that I didn't realize Anita was headed straight for me as she walked into the wings, letting one foot drift into my path.

I couldn't react fast enough to stop. I tripped, falling hard onto my forearms, the blunt pain radiating up into my palms and knees.

"Hey!" I cried out in surprise, but it barely seemed to faze Anita at all.

"Watch it, kid," she snarled, glaring down at me from on high. I moved my lips wordlessly, like a fish. She laughed at me, and it was an ugly, mean laugh. "No use lip-syncing back here, booger."

I didn't know what she meant, but I could tell it was an insult. The awkward pause in the show was palpable—I had to get on stage! I struggled to get back up on my heels as Anita strode past without stopping. Aida Lott rushed over to help me up.

"Ignore her," she said. "She thinks she's all that and a bucket of KFC. Just shake it off, baby girl. The audience didn't see. Get out there!"

I nodded, too flustered to reply. All I could do was straighten my wig, take a deep breath—

And take my first steps into the light.

Painfully bright, white light. I fought the urge to raise a hand to shield my eyes. I could barely make out any faces, just bobbing, shadowy silhouettes and flashes of smiles. I heard clapping, but it was muffled by the sound of my heartbeat pounding in my ears, deafening me: *tha-RUMP tha-RUMP tha-RUMP.*

One foot in front of the other, one step at a time, I made my way down the stage toward the audience. My heels pounded the floor with a sharp *CLICK-CLACK-CLACK,* their silver glitter refracting light all around the room like a disco ball.

RuPaul sang out over the sound system, and I thought, *Yes, okay, I'm doing it*! I reached the lip of the stage, placed one hand on my hip, and *POP!* I shifted my weight to one side, just like Tío Billy had taught me.

The audience cheered, and I heard shouts of "Yaaas!" and "O-*kay!*" and "Work!" As I turned to make my way back up stage, Mom's wordless hollering and Tío Billy calling out, "Yes, Miss Lottie!" cut through the noise. Emboldened by their cheers, I closed my eyes, turned my face up toward the hot stage lights and threw one arm in the air, feeling every inch like . . . well, like a queen.

With a big, goofy grin on my face, I ducked back into the darkness of the wings, panting for breath.

Aida Lott was waiting for me and scooped me up into a big hug the moment I was offstage. "Well, that was fierce!" she said, giving me a squeeze. "Congrats, little Lottie; you're officially a drag queen! Welcome to the club."

You're officially a drag queen. Her words rumbled again and again in my head like delicious thunder. *Whoa. I am. I really am.*

"Come on!" I looked around for the familiar voice, and Tío Billy's face appeared at the stage door, illuminated from behind. "We have to go!"

I had been enjoying being Lottie so much, I had almost forgotten that the night wasn't even close to over. I looked from Tío Billy to Aida.

"Sorry," I said to Aida, "I have to run. It was

super nice meeting you!" And I kicked off my heels, scooped them up, and dashed toward the door, my other hand keeping my wig in place as I ran.

"León!" Tío Billy exclaimed as we rushed up the stairs to meet Mom. "You were just as fabulous as you were at home. Even better!"

"Thanks!" I shouted over the sound of us bolting toward Hoosier Mama's entrance. "I can't believe I just did that!"

"Start believing, león!" he cried as we burst through the front doors. Mom had the engine running, parked right out front. We sprinted for the car, flinging open the doors. "Gun it!" he hollered as we dove inside. Mom threw the car into drive and stepped on the gas, peeling away.

"Baby, you were incredible!" she cried from behind the wheel.

"Honestly, león, we're going to run out of words to describe it," Tío Billy said from the passenger seat. "I'd hug you but I don't want to ruin your makeup!"

"Don't worry about it," I panted. "It all has to come off anyway." I reached behind me and unzipped my dress.

"Come off?" Tío Billy asked. "It can't come off! Not if you're going to do another round."

"What?" I asked, reeling. "What are you talking about?"

"There won't be time to do your face all over

again, león," Tío Billy said, rummaging around his feet for my backpack. "This first round will last about a half an hour, then there's an hour break, then the next round starts. We'll be lucky if we can make it back in time, much less do your makeup."

"Are you serious? Look at me!" Tío Billy tossed me my uniform as I waved a hand over my face. "I can't go to Mathletes like this!"

"Why can't he take it off? Is it really that big of a deal?" Mom reasoned, putting on her turn signal to merge into traffic. I wrangled the dress over my head with difficulty, struggling against its weight.

"He could," Tío Billy hedged, chewing his lip. "Pero queens . . . no hacen eso. It's just not done. Everyone else will be pulling out all the stops."

"Well, who cares what everyone else is doing?" Mom scoffed.

"I do!" I wailed. My heart had begun to race, my fingers trembling as I worked on the buttons of my white shirt. "I'll get laughed off the stage if I'm not painted!"

"No one would laugh at you," Tío Billy said firmly. "Not if they ever want to be invited back to Hoosier Mama, I can tell you that much."

"And that's just if you make it to the next round," Mom said. "Maybe you won't, and then you won't have to worry about it!"

"Is that supposed to make me feel better?" I

cried, trying to pull my head through my sweater vest without covering the clothes in makeup. "I *want* to make it to the next round!"

"Okay, león," Tío Billy said, his firm voice cutting through my rising hysteria. "I want you to remember something. You, Martin McLean, are not defined by what those kids think of you, just like Lottie isn't defined by her makeup." He reached back to place a reassuring hand on my knee. "Whatever you decide, your fierceness is going to shine through. You know why? Because there's more of you in Lottie than the other way around."

I couldn't respond; my lungs felt like they were on fire from repressing a sob. I wanted so badly to cry, and I was clenching my jaw so hard that it hurt.

"Take a second to think about it. We'll support you, no matter what," he said, passing back the remaining contents of my backpack: a comb, a little mirror, and a pack of makeup wipes.

You don't get it, Tío Billy, I wanted to say. *Don't you know how middle schoolers are?* All it would take is for one person to declare me a freak, and the rest would follow. Looking raggedy in Round Two would be nothing compared to spending the rest of my school years as a social pariah. If I showed up to Mathletes looking like Lottie, my life would be over. My life, and Lottie's too. As much as I loved performing as Lottie, how could I ever be brave enough to take the stage again in the face of all that ridicule? If my classmates found out about Lottie, I could lose her forever.

I took a deep breath . . . and wiped the makeup off my face.

☆ 13 ☆

I arrived at Baker's Lake Academy smack dab in the middle of the Patented Pickle Plan.

Once Mom slammed on her brakes in the parking lot, I leapt out of the car and rushed into the auditorium. As I pushed open the heavy double doors, Pickle's voice rang out from the center of the room.

"Help, help! Is there a doctor on board?" he cried. He was waving his hands around, gesturing wildly to Violet, who was slumped back in her wheelchair. "Anybody, help!"

A small crowd began to form around Pickle and Violet. I ran down the aisle and pushed my way through to them.

"Tone. It. Down!" Violet hissed at Pickle, her head turned away from the crowd.

"Give her some room, people!" Pickle yelled,

waving his arms around as though he were landing a plane. "Let her breathe!"

"Pickle!" I whispered, making a "cut it out" motion with my hand across my neck. He caught my eye and grinned.

Mr. Berg, the Baker's Lake Academy coach, came jogging down the aisle in his sweater vest with two school nurses at his side, Carmen following close behind. Pickle began to howl.

"Someone, help her! She's just a child!"

"Here!" Carmen cried. "I got Mr. Berg! Let us through!"

The crowd parted, and the nurses swept over to Violet. As they checked her pulse, Mr. Berg mopped sweat from his forehead with a handkerchief.

"What happened?" he asked Pickle. Carmen sidled up next to me and poked me in the side, tilting her head toward the action with a giggle. I shook my head in disbelief.

"Oh, woe betide me, sir!" Pickle said, wringing his hands. I swear I saw Mr. Berg roll his eyes. "One second she was telling me how incredibly handsome I am—"

It was *my* turn to roll my eyes.

"—and the next, she was hyperventilating! I tried to calm her down, but she fainted! My good looks were too much for her, sir, but I swear I did everything I could to help."

Violet stirred next to us, groaning and looking

around groggily. She caught my eye for the briefest moment and almost smiled despite the act.

"Wh-where am I?" she asked, faking total dis-orientation.

"You're at Baker's Lake Academy," I said helpfully. Mr. Berg turned to look at me, startled.

"Oh, Martin," he said, "you're here." He looked at my face strangely, then shook his head. "You should get backstage. Mr. Peterson has been looking for you."

"What happened?" Violet asked weakly.

"It seems you may have fainted," Mr. Berg said gently. "We're going to take you to the nurse's office, okay?"

Violet nodded and began to navigate herself up the aisle—there was no point in stalling any longer since I was there. Pickle leapt in front of them and started running ahead, swinging his arms wildly.

"Make way! Make way, people! We've got a sick girl coming through!" With a rush of zeal, he kicked open the auditorium doors to let Violet through.

Then he turned his head to us and winked.

"Incredible," I murmured. "That *worked?*"

"You have to go!" Carmen exclaimed, wheeling me toward the back of the auditorium. "We've only bought you a few minutes."

"I know," I said, stopping just shy of the backstage entrance. "Carmen, thank you. And thank Pickle and Violet for me too."

"Thank us after you're the first ever drag show/
Mathletes double champion!" she said. "Now hurry!"

And with that, I ducked backstage. As my eyes
adjusted to the relative darkness I saw the team
huddled around Mr. Peterson, their bodies etched
with worry. I cleared my throat. Mr. Peterson whirled
around, then looked as though he might crumple
with relief.

"Martin!" he exclaimed. "Thank goodness."

"Where have you been?" Poppy demanded.

"We were super worried," Chris said. Then he
cocked his head at me, his brow furrowing. "Are you
okay?"

"Hi," I said. "I-I'm really sorry I'm late. I . . . had
to be somewhere."

"Where, the freak show?" Nelson cackled from
the back of the group. "You look like a Party City
barfed all over you, McLean!"

"What are you talking about?" I asked, suddenly
filled with dread.

"You're covered in glitter!" Nelson wheezed
through his laughter.

I raised my hand to my face. Hot pink glitter
came off on my fingers. *Oh, no.*

"It's—it's nothing!" I stammered, rubbing my
face as hard as I could. A thousand little flecks of
sparkle fell onto my hand. *The car was too dark,* I
realized with a sickening twist in my gut. *I didn't get*

all the glitter off. I heard giggles in the group, and my face turned hot.

"*It's nothing!*" Nelson mocked, pointing. "It's *glitter*! *Pink* glitter! What happened to you, McLean? Did you join Cirque du So-Gay?"

The lies came to mind all at once: *Carmen's glitter pens exploded on me. The Baker's Lake Academy cheerleading squad passed me in the hall and beat me up. A cyclone hit the glitter aisle at the crafts store, and then it landed on my house!*

For once, I had thought of a million things to say. But they all felt wrong. Instead, I heard Tío Billy's voice in my head: *Your life, león, is one fabulous show. Don't miss out on it.*

And I knew what I had to do.

I had lied so much to keep Lottie a secret, but I didn't want to anymore. No lie would keep Nelson from harassing me. The truth wouldn't stop him either. But at least if I told the truth, I would be free. No more hiding, no more lying. I could just *be.*

I was scared—really scared—that all my teammates would abandon me, that I'd be teased and bullied until eighth grade graduation and beyond. But if I lied, I'd be abandoning Lottie. I'd be abandoning myself. And that would be scarier than anything Nelson could throw at me.

So I looked him in the eye and said the only thing I could:

"Actually, I'm a drag queen."

Nelson's mouth hung open as though it had come unhinged. Mariam and Poppy were looking at one another with wide eyes. I couldn't bring myself to look at Chris.

"What?" Nelson asked, shocked laughter rising in his voice.

"I'm. A. Drag. Queen." I said, enunciating every word. "I came from a show. A *drag* show," I added, for emphasis. "I'm Lottie León. Though that's *Miss* León to you." I felt a rush of shock and pride. *Where did that come from*?!

Nelson didn't get a chance to reply. At that moment, Mr. Berg came hurrying backstage and approached Mr. Peterson.

"I'm sorry for the delay. There was an . . . incident," Mr. Berg said, sighing heavily. "Let's get this going, shall we?"

"Dan, wait," Mr. Peterson said, gesturing toward me. "Can we have a minute, please? I think my captain might like a chance to wash his face." I nodded emphatically behind him.

"There's no time," Mr. Berg said. "We're already behind schedule, we have to keep things moving."

"Well, then there's nothing to be done," Mr. Peterson said grimly as Mr. Berg left to gather his team. "You're just going to have to go on." I swallowed hard against the lump in my throat.

"You're going to let him compete like that?" asked J.P. "I'm sorry, Mr. P, but that's bonkers! He looks like a disco ball!"

"It's ridiculous," Nelson concurred, crossing his arms. Mr. Peterson shot him a warning look.

"I'm ashamed of you all," he said, and everyone became very still. "I never took you to be the kind of students who would lash out against a teammate just because he looks different. Martin is your captain. Would you really risk losing Regionals and letting your teammates down—letting *me* down, and your parents, too, no doubt—over a little glitter?"

Mr. Peterson stared at the group. Everyone was quiet, until Mariam shook her head.

"No," she said. "No, of course not."

"Yeah," Konrad agreed after a moment. "Who cares? Your brain still works, doesn't it, Martin?" I nodded, surprised. "See? What does it matter what he looks like if he can still compete?"

"Drag is kind of rock and roll, actually!" Poppy exclaimed.

"He has to compete," Chris said, looking at me with kind eyes. "He's our captain."

"He wasn't even supposed to be our captain in the first place!" J.P. burst out, his face contorted in outrage. "It should have been me, or Chris, or both, because we've got seniority. Not this cross-dressing freak!"

"Hey!" Chris said sharply, turning to his brother. "Knock it off! You were never going to be captain. Stop taking it out on Martin!"

"What, like he isn't asking for it, showing up looking like that? It's so weird!" J.P. exclaimed. He waved his arms at me as though my very presence proved his point. "He's obviously not fit to be captain. I'm with Nelson."

Chris flashed J.P. an angry glare. "Jeez, I thought Mom and Dad raised you better than this," Chris said, "but I guess I'm the only Cregg twin with a heart *or* a brain."

"I—wha—you—hey!" J.P. stuttered. Chris cocked his head toward me.

"Nobody insults my friends, J.P. Not even my brother. Apologize to Martin," he said. "Now."

J.P. cast a bewildered look at his brother, then at Mr. Peterson, then at Nelson, and finally at me. He bit the inside of his cheek and pouted.

"I'm sorry, Martin," he mumbled. "You can compete with us, I guess. Whatever. I don't care."

"How heartfelt," Chris said sarcastically. He smiled at me gently. "I'm sorry, Martin. We want you to compete with us."

Mr. Peterson turned his gaze on Nelson, who kept his arms crossed over his chest in contempt.

"What say you, Mr. Turlington? Bearing in mind that the majority has already overruled your opinion," he said, and I swear I caught him stifling a smile. Nelson scowled.

"Whatever," he spat. "It's your funeral."

"Your approval is noted," Mr. Peterson said dryly, then clapped his hands together. "Very well! Martin, take your place at the front of the group. It's almost time."

I stood at the head of the line and waited for the announcer to call our team. *Well, if nothing else, no one will forget that you were captain,* I thought.

As we took our places, the moderator, a middle-aged man with stringy gray hair and beady eyes, peered at me from over his tiny glasses. I watched the kids on the Baker's Lake Academy team whisper, but to my surprise, no tears sprang to my eyes. I was . . . fine. I was better than fine, actually. It wasn't bothering me! *Let them whisper. Let them stare. I'm here to win, not worry about their opinions.*

Chris nudged me from the podium next to mine.

"Let's do this," he whispered, and my heart soared. The moderator was looking offstage to our coaches, but Mr. Peterson frowned and gestured for him to continue.

"Okay, then. Welcome to this year's Junior Mathletes Regional Competition. Our competitors today are Meadow Crest Junior High and Baker's Lake Academy. This will be a contest in three rounds, the first, a sprint round . . ."

All thoughts of wayward sparkles melted away. I breezed through the sprint and target rounds, and during the team round, even Nelson deferred to me. Which meant that, as we headed into the sudden death round, we were doing better than we ever had before—but we were still tied with Baker's Lake.

"We now begin the tiebreaker," the moderator said into his microphone. "This is a sudden death round. Each team will play one individual. The competitors from each team will be verbally posed a problem. They will have four minutes to either submit an answer or pass. If both competitors pass, we will move on to another question. Likewise, if both competitors submit a correct answer, we will move on to another question. The first individual to submit a correct answer against their competitor's incorrect answer or pass wins. Do the teams understand?"

"Yes," we all replied in unison.

"Good," the moderator replied. "The teams have one minute to select your competitor. Time begins now."

"It's up to you, Martin," Mariam whispered. "You're the best at these."

"I don't know," I said, eyeing the competition. Lucas O'Connor, a Baker's Lake eighth grader, stared right back at me. "They look ready for a fight. Are you sure you want me? Maybe Chris would be better . . ."

"No way," Chris said. "You're great in a final round. You finish the job."

"Time is up," the moderator announced. "Have the teams selected their competitors?"

"Yes," Lucas said, stepping up to the Baker's Lake podium. I swallowed hard and approached our podium.

"Yes," I replied. "We have."

"Very well, then. We begin the sudden death round," the moderator said. "The first question: Pump A can drain a swimming pool in four hours. Pump B can drain a swimming pool in six hours. Both pumps started to drain the same pool at 8 a.m. An hour later, Pump B breaks down. Pump B takes one hour to repair, and is started up again. When will the pool be empty?"

My mind went serenely quiet as I put pencil to paper. The figures lined themselves up like dance steps, tangoing to the tune of my cat-scratch writing. *Pump A has been operating for an hour in when Pump B breaks down, meaning it has been working for two hours by the time Pump B is restarted. . . .* I looked up at Lucas, who was grimacing. *But Pump B also worked for an hour,* I realized. *And when it starts back up, the two parts will work even better in unison.* A rush of victory filled me. I saw the clock ticking away out of the corner of my eye, bright red numbers flickering. I finished my calculations, heart *tha-RUMP*-ing, and put my pencil down.

"Time!" The moderator called. "Meadow Crest Junior High, do you have an answer?"

"Yes," I replied, my heart filling with anticipation, "10:48 a.m."

Tha-RUMP tha-RUMP tha-RUMP.

"Baker's Lake Academy, do you have an answer?"

Tha-RUMP tha-RUMP tha-RUMP.

"Yes," Lucas said. "11:12 a.m."

11:12 a.m.? I thought. *That can't be right. Can it? No, I checked my work. 11:12 a.m. is too long—Lucas forgot that Pump B had already worked for an hour before it broke down.*

And if he forgot, does that mean—?

The moderator checked his answer sheet as the room held its breath. He looked back up at Lucas, then at me.

Tha-RUMP tha-RUMP tha-RUMP.

Tha-RUMP tha-RUMP tha-RUMP.

THA-RUMP THA-RUMP THA-RUMP.

"The correct answer is 10:48 a.m. Meadow Crest Junior High is the winner."

The room erupted.

All at once my team was surrounding me, throwing their arms around me and screaming, jumping up and down and crying.

"WE WON!" Mariam yelled, "WE FREAKING WON!"

"Baker's Lake can suck it!"

"*Poppy*!"

"Sorry, Mr. P!" Poppy hollered, pumping her fist in the air. "BUT WE WON!"

Behind me, Konrad started singing an uncharacteristically raucous rendition of "We Are the Champions," his arms flung around J.P. and Nelson.

"You did it! Martin, you did it!" Chris was in front of me in the throng, his face positively glowing. Behind him, the Baker's Lake team was stoically watching the chaos, arms crossed over their chests.

Mr. Peterson made his way to the front and accepted the massive golden trophy from the moderator. He hoisted it over his head, and we all cheered loud enough to make my ears ring. Then Mr. Peterson handed me the trophy with a hearty pat on the back.

"It's yours, captain," he said, and I swore even his elbow patches looked proud. "And so is the microphone. Say a few words?"

The speech. For the first time since making it to the podium, my throat went tight. I hadn't prepared a speech, not a single word. The crowd parted, the team all smiles, and Mr. Berg came forward to lower the standing microphone for me. I looked out onto the sea of people, all of whom were looking back at me in all my glittery glory. I cleared my throat.

"Um," I began, and the reverberation of my

voice against the auditorium walls startled me. From the back of the room, I heard a distinctly Pickle-like voice give a "Woo!"

"Thank you," I said. "Um. My name is Martin McLean, and I'm the captain of the Meadow Crest Junior Mathletes team." I looked over to the team, who nodded encouragingly. I took a shaky breath and continued.

"I would really like to give a speech, especially because I've been dreaming about this moment for . . . well, basically for my entire life," I said. "But—"

I looked out into the audience, and saw Mom running up the aisle as Tío Billy waved his hands over his head.

"YOU: ROUND TWO," he mouthed, holding two fingers up in the air. "GOTTA GO." He pantomimed running and cocked his head violently toward the door. Next to him, Pickle and Carmen hopped up and down frantically.

"But I have to go?" I asked, into the microphone. There were gasps from behind me and murmurs in the crowd. Out in the audience, Tío Billy nodded. *Oh my God. I made it to the next round!*

"But I have to go!" I yelped. "Oh, man, I'm—I'm really sorry. I have to go. Sorry! Thank you! But, yeah, gotta go. Bye. Sorry! Bye!"

I stepped back from the microphone to a

smattering of applause. The team swarmed around me, shouting questions, but I pushed through the throng with the trophy and ran off the stage into the audience.

"Wait, Martin!" Mr. Peterson was following me, with the rest of the team trailing close behind. "What's the matter? You can't go; we have to celebrate!"

"I want to stay, I really do," I said, handing the trophy back to him. "But there's somewhere I have to be."

"Where?" Poppy demanded.

"It's another competition," I said.

"Another one?" Konrad exclaimed.

"The same one," I stuttered. "I mean, the one I was at before. The drag show. It's a competition, and I made it to the final round, but it's happening, like, *now.*"

I turned to see Mom and Tío Billy flying down the aisle toward us, flanked by Pickle, Carmen, and Violet.

"León, we have to hustle," Tío Billy said, waving me toward the door. "Dorie texted; she put you at the very end of the lineup, but we're never going to make it unless we leave"—he checked the time on his phone—"Five minutes ago!"

"But my makeup!"

"You're just going to have to go on without it,"

he said. "I can't get you made up in that car, not with the way your mother drives."

"Then I'll lose for sure!" I wailed. "I might as well not even show up!"

"That's not true!" Carmen said. "You have to go, Martin, you've worked so hard."

"She's right, mijo," Mom said. "I didn't raise you to give up!"

"No," I said, shaking my head. A powerful lump was forming in my throat. "I can't. This . . . this was supposed to be Lottie's big performance. It has to be perfect. Without her makeup . . ." I hung my head, tears pricking in my eyes. *It's over.*

"Wait!" Chris stepped forward, a gleam in his blue eyes. "We can help."

"What?"

"The team! We can help you get ready," he said. "We'll take the Mathletes bus. It's the perfect mobile get-ready station. And Mr. Peterson's the smoothest driver around!"

Mr. Peterson straightened the hem of his sweater bashfully, going pink beneath the collar.

"Thank you, Mr. Cregg," he said. "I'd be happy to help, but only if everyone's folks are okay with a little detour."

"Oh, I am *all* over it," Mariam said, whipping out her phone to start texting the team phone tree and notify everyone's parents.

"This is perfect!" Carmen exclaimed, whirling around to face me. "Your tío Billy and your Mom can go ahead of us in her car. That way if they beat us there, they can make sure Dorie holds the show for you!"

"Ay, no way, I'm too nervous to drive! I'll go in the bus with you and help with makeup. I know a thing or two about painting," Mom said. She tossed Tío Billy her keys.

"Anybody else want to ride ahead?" he asked.

"We'll go," Chris said, grabbing J.P. by the arm.

"Hey!" J.P. protested.

"Somebody should be there to save seats for the team so we can support Martin," Chris said pointedly. "It's the least we can do."

"You guys," I said, looking around at the group. Tears of gratitude sprung to my eyes. "I . . . I can't believe you'd do this for me."

"Of course!" Poppy exclaimed. "You think we'd let our team captain down?"

"You showed up for us," Chris said earnestly. "Now we can do the same for you."

"You can't do this!" Nelson said. "That bus is my ride back to Bloomington!"

"Tough," Poppy said, sticking out her tongue. "Call a cab if you don't like it. I'm sure your mommy and daddy will pay for it." Nelson grit his teeth.

"I maxed out my allowance for the month already, Poppy," he hissed. "You *know* that."

"Then it looks like you're stuck with us!" Chris said with a chipper grin.

"Well, Martin? Shall we get this show on the road?" Mr. Peterson asked.

I looked to Tío Billy, sure he'd tell me it was too late, we wasted too much time, kiss my drag queen dreams goodbye. But instead he hooted, and threw his hands up in the air.

"Ay, middle-schoolers!" he laughed. "I never know what to expect. Okay, then! Vámonos!"

"Let's move, people!" Pickle crowed. "We've got a queen to crown!"

☆ 14 ☆

I might be the first drag queen in history to have been on the receiving end of a false lash application while traveling at 70 miles per hour down the Interstate.

As we squealed out of the parking lot, a makeup wipe hit me in the face with a *THWAP!*

"Hold still!" Carmen scolded, wiping my face ferociously as she pinned me into my seat.

"I'm trying!" I coughed. "You're getting it in my mouth!"

"Well, that has to be clean, too, so buck up!"

"Martin, where's your dress?" Mariam yelled from the back. "We should get you in it before they do your makeup! Poppy, do you want me to tuck some napkins into his collar, just in case?"

"Just in case?" Poppy protested, rifling through Tío Billy's cosmetics bag. "I once completed a self-portrait using nothing but an eyebrow pencil and my wits. I'll have you know I am *extremely* careful!"

"You're going to be doing liquid eyeliner in a moving vehicle," Mariam replied. "Most professionals can't even do that!"

"She's right," Mom said to Poppy. "We need all the precautions we can get. The dress and jacket are in this garment bag," she instructed Mariam, handing it over by its hanger. "Shoes and wig are in these boxes. Wig comb is in the little pocket in my purse."

"Uh, Ms. Perez?" Konrad asked, huddled over the backpack with Mariam. "How do I work these?" He held up a pair of sheer pantyhose, tangled into a ball. In the corner of the back seat, Nelson turned red and looked away.

"They're for under the dress," Mariam laughed, snatching them out of his hands and passing them to Violet, whose chair had been secured in place with a series of safety belts. "Let a professional deal with those."

"On it!" Violet said, getting to work. "Martin, are you sure you don't want to switch your look up? Maybe go for some purple lips? Or, ooh, purple glitter!"

"But who could wear purple as well as you, my darling?" Pickle asked, spinning my wig on one finger.

"Aw, you're sweet!" Violet beamed.

"Ay, stop that!" Mom cried, wagging a finger at Pickle, who went a little pale. "Give me a minute and I'll help you with the comb. No twirling!"

"Yes, ma'am."

"Poppy? His face is clean," Carmen said. "Let's do this."

"Okay, ladies, here's what we're going for," Mom said, pulling up the reference photo Tío Billy had texted her. "Just ask if you need my help. Pickle?" she asked, turning to him. "Let's start on the wig."

"Martin, close your eyes," Poppy demanded, brandishing a foundation sponge like a scalpel.

"Wait, the dress!" Mariam wailed. "Arms over your head, Martin, now!"

I was plunged into Lottie's gown, beads smacking me in the face and arms as I went. No sooner was I zipped in than Poppy attacked me with her sponge, dabbing on primer, foundation, and concealer. *This is unbelievable,* I thought, as Violet lifted one of my feet to start rolling on my pantyhose. *Unbelievable and totally amazing.*

"Stop smiling!" Poppy protested. "You'll make your under-eyes crease!"

"Time check?" Carmen hollered. "What's our ETA?"

"Ten minutes!" Mom replied.

"Make that eight," Mr. Peterson added, stepping on the gas.

"Just got a text from Chris!" Pickle called.

"And?" I asked, as Poppy combed through my eyebrows. Chris, J.P., and Tío Billy had taken off for Hoosier Mama while we were still loading up the bus.

"He says they're almost there," Pickle replied, "and they're prepared to throw elbows if the need arises."

"He did *not* actually say that, Peter," Violet scolded.

"Well, okay. But he *should* be prepared to knock someone into the Forgotten Realms if they get in Martin's way, is all I'm saying."

A nervous thrill ran through me. In a matter of minutes, Chris would see me in full drag as Lottie. What would he think? What would he *say*? It was one thing to know that I'm a drag queen—and another to actually see it. But there was no time dwell on it—we were hurtling toward my future in a bus emblazoned with algebraic equations, and there was no turning back.

"Hand me the eye shadow palette."

"Got it!" Carmen passed the palette over to Poppy with a nervous giggle.

"Great, get the lash glue going. Martin, are you very attached to your eyelashes?"

"Who needs 'em?" I replied cheerfully.

"That's what I like to hear. Aaand, here we go!"

★ ★ ★

The bus came flying to a screeching halt in the Hoosier Mama parking lot. The second we were stationary, Mom rushed over to me. With the team gathered around us, she surveyed Lottie's final look.

"Lashes on, hair laid, dress zipped . . ." She smiled wide and handed me her compact mirror. "It's all perfect, baby!"

I examined my face anxiously, trying to ferret out any imperfections that could lead to drag disaster. *For a face done by a bunch of middle schoolers in the back of a moving bus, this is pretty incredible,* I thought, brushing a curl off my forehead. *But something's missing . . .*

"It's *almost* perfect," I said. "But . . . Poppy, could you hand me the brown eyeliner?" Poppy whipped out the eyeliner and handed it to me dutifully. Taking the pencil from her, I carefully dotted my cheek just once. "Can't forget my beauty mark," I said, checking my work in the mirror. "Cassie Blanca would insist, and so do I."

I closed the compact and looked up to see Mom fighting back tears.

"You look beautiful, mijo," she said proudly. "But you have to go! You're on any second!"

The group parted to let me through as I made my way to the front of the bus. Mr. Peterson flung the door open, but I couldn't move. I spun around and faced the group.

"You guys," I began. "I don't know how to thank you—"

"GO!" Everyone hollered.

So I hurried off the bus with the team hot on my heels, up Hoosier Mama's porch and through the front door. The coffee shop was deserted; everyone was in the basement for the show. I ran downstairs and tried to keep my thoughts from racing too: *Stay calm. Remember what Tío Billy said: there's more of you in Lottie than the other way around. You can do this.*

Halfway down the stairs, I saw the crowd of people packed into the basement studio like beef in a pastelito. Dorie's voice echoed over the speakers.

"Next up is our pint-size prima donna, our middle school queen. At just twelve years old, she is . . . Lottie León!"

"Yo Viviré" began pouring out of the sound system. The lights came up on stage, but I wasn't there. I was at the bottom of the stairs, trying to figure out how I was going to make my way through the throng, until—I saw Chris holding back the crowd on one side, J.P. pushing people back on the other.

"Come on, Martin!" Chris called over his shoulder at me. "You're on!"

I closed my eyes and took a breath. I was going onstage alone, but not by myself.

A path was cleared, my song was playing, and there was only one thing left to do. I ran up the center aisle, already mouthing the words. *Bom bom bom-bom!* went the music as I leapt onstage. I raised my hands up over my head, my back to the audience, and cascaded them down in a rain of spirit fingers, just like Tío Billy taught me. Then, with a flourish and a shimmy, I turned to face the crowd.

Einstein gave the world a very important theory: the theory of relativity. He imagined the fabric of space and time bending—time literally being slowed—as it flowed around objects with a strong gravity field. It means that time moves like molasses around the largest stars, the densest planets.

And in the moment my friends saw me on stage, glittering under the lights, performing in full drag, time stopped around me. I was a star, with my own field of gravity.

The split-second of silence seemed to last forever, then: The cheer that rose up was deafening. The team was up on their feet, shouting and whistling and clapping. If there was any nervousness left in my body, it vanished when I saw them. I couldn't make out faces, but I knew they were there. Mom and Tío Billy were there too, Mom's wolf-like whooping piercing through the music and applause.

It was as if the choreography had been woven into my muscles: *Side cross step! Side cross step! Shimmy down, shimmy back.* My brain was barely part of the equation; my hips and hands seemed to move of their own accord. I was smiling as I lip-synced, which probably ruined the illusion a little, but I couldn't help it and I didn't care. My entire body was lit up by starlight, or pure electricity, or both.

Reedy trumpets signaled the instrumental break. I did my spins, being careful to "spot" a place on the back wall so I didn't get dizzy. One, two, three, four tight twirls across the full expanse of the stage! From the spins, Celia's voice returned, and *BAM!* Into my cross to stage right!

The crowd was on their feet, clapping along, reaching out their hands when I got close to them onstage. I don't remember if I posed correctly, or got every word of the song right, but it didn't matter. Nothing mattered, really, except the feeling in my heart and the music in my ears. I hit my final pose, panting for breath. My face felt like it would break from smiling, like it was about to shatter into a million pieces on the floor.

And just like that, it was over.

The house lights rose, and I saw Pickle standing on his chair, clapping as hard as he could. Violet was whistling while Carmen bounced up and down, beaming. From the end of the row, Chris waved, the disco lights swirling like snow across his face, lighting up his freckles. I grinned and waved back.

"That's our girl! Lottie León, everybody!" Dorie said over the microphone. I took another bow, and another, waving to my team and Tío Billy, who was beaming, and Mom, who was crying. I could have stayed out there forever, memorizing every cheer, every face, every feeling to keep in my memory, but I had to leave the stage. Still catching my breath, I reluctantly turned and ducked into the wings.

Backstage, Aida Lott rushed me, picking me up off the ground and spinning me around.

"Come through, little Lottie! You *killed* it, girl!" she squealed, setting me back down. "And that song choice, so fierce!"

"Thanks, Aida! You made it to the final round too?"

Aida nodded, then leaned in close.

"You missed it! That shady mess over there?" She cocked her head toward the stage door, where Anita Paycheck sat perched on a stool, pouting. "Kitty girl choked. Forgot her routine halfway through Britney's 'Toxic.'" Aida pulled a "yikes" face. "That's what she gets for messing with Miss Lottie León's big debut, am I right?" She nudged me with her elbow and giggled.

After a few minutes of anxious waiting

backstage, Dorie's voice once again rang out over the sound system.

"Weren't all our queens fabulous?" Dorie asked, to many cheers. "Now it's time to welcome them back to the stage for our awards ceremony." A hush began to fall over the crowd. "I repeat, all queens back on stage for the awards ceremony."

I sucked in my breath. *This is it*! Aida took my hand excitedly and guided me back on stage. She and I took our places next to three other queens, including Anita. Dorie put on suspenseful music and then made her way onstage, mic in one hand and a slip of paper in the other.

"The time has come," she said, tossing her locs over one shoulder and wiggling her eyebrows suggestively. "These five fabulous queens have worked and twerked for the gods, and your response has helped decide who will take home the crown."

I was so nervous, I could feel my teeth vibrating. *Tha-RUMP tha-RUMP tha-RUMP* went my heart, pounding so hard it hurt. Aida Lott squeezed my sweaty hand tight. "In fifth place . . . Anita Paycheck!"

Anita sulked forward, met with lukewarm applause. Even though she had been shady—and downright mean—during the competition, I felt a little sorry for Anita. *I can't blame her for being disappointed,* I thought. *Who would be happy to come in last?*

Anita shook Dorie's hand and exited, shooting daggers with her eyes at those of us left on stage. Dorie cleared her throat.

Tha-RUMP tha-RUMP tha-RUMP.

"In fourth place . . . Miss Pennie Dreadfulle!"

An Asian queen with short-cropped raven hair, wire-rimmed glasses, and scarlet lipstick bounded forward, took a big bow, then sashayed offstage. In the audience, I saw Mom mouth "TOP. THREE!" I couldn't breathe.

Tha-RUMP tha-RUMP tha-RUMP

"In third place . . ."

Please not me please not me please not me please not me—

". . . Lottie León!"

For a split second, my stomach sank. *I didn't win,* I realized, a dull roar rushing in my ears. *I got third.* Then the world came back into focus, and people were cheering, and Dorie was hugging me tight.

"You were wonderful, sugar," she whispered in my ear, pressing her soft face against mine. She placed a red sash over my head and handed me a little tiara encrusted with crystals and ruby red jewels. "Be proud!"

"GO LOTTIE!" Pickle yelled from atop his chair.

"THAT'S OUR CAPTAIN!" Poppy called out.

"THAT'S MY BABY!" Mom cried in response,

eliciting warm laughter and even more applause.

"Take a bow, león!" Tío Billy shouted. Dorie stepped aside and gestured to me with a smile. I stepped forward and bowed, then raised my tiara in the air and whooped for joy, loud as any lion on the plains.

★ ★ ★

Aida Lott won first place.

As soon as she came offstage, covered in confetti and wearing her massive crown, I ran over to her.

"Congratulations!" I said, throwing my arms around her waist. "You deserve it."

"I don't know, Miss León, you gave me a run for my money!" she said, pulling away gently to smile at my sash. "I think next time you're going to be the one to beat. You should be very happy with that performance, chickadee." I beamed back up at her.

"I am." *I really am.*

It didn't matter that I didn't take first, I realized. It didn't matter at all. What mattered was that when I was onstage, I didn't worry about anything. I didn't worry about saying the wrong thing or about what Dad would have said or about bullies like Nelson.

Instead, I just basked in being me: Martin McLean, middle school queen, *and* Martin McLean, champion Mathletes captain. I didn't need anyone's approval—I could be anyone I wanted to be.

And that was worth *way* more than a crown.

"C'mon," Aida said, taking my hand. "Let's get out of these get-ups so you can go greet your adoring fans!"

After I changed into my street clothes and removed as much of the makeup as I could, I ducked out into the slowly dissipating audience—and ran smack-dab into Carmen.

"MARTIN!" she shrieked, tackling me. "That was the most amazing thing I've ever *seen!* Are you just *dying*? Were you nervous? Was it fun? Do your feet hurt? Are those lights as bright as they seem?"

"Give the guy a chance to breathe, Carmen!" Pickle said, sidling up with Violet. "That, my friend, was pretty hardcore. Now, if you had taken home the thousand bucks, well—"

"Peter!" Violet scolded. Pickle gave a sheepish grin.

"What I mean to say is . . . you're awesome, dude."

"Love you too, Pickle," I said.

Violet smiled sweetly at me. "Martin, you're so talented! I had no idea you could dance."

"Neither did I," I admitted.

"Maybe you could give Peter a few lessons," she said, leaning her head against Pickle's arm.

He pretended to scowl. "We'll see about that."

"Ooh!" Carmen exclaimed, her eyes lighting up.

"There's Aida Lott! I'm going to go say hi. I want to know *all* about her artistic process."

She glided toward the back of the room, where the Mathletes were gathered around Aida, Dorie, and a few of the queens who hadn't made it past the first round. Poppy and Mariam were deep in animated conversation with Aida when Carmen butted in.

"I'm Carmen Miranda, yes, like the fruit lady," she said by way of introduction. Nearby, Mr. Peterson, having been cornered by the busty redheaded queen who came in second, was visibly sweating and turning the color of a fire hydrant. Even J.P. and Nelson were politely, if nervously, talking to Anita Paycheck, who seemed to have mellowed somewhat since her defeat.

Chris appeared on the edge of the group. Finally seeing him in the light, my butterflies started up again. He waved me over with a freckled hand. Suddenly shy, I made my way to him. *Play it cool, Martin,* I thought. *It's no big deal. Nope, no big deal at all. Definitely not a big deal that Chris just saw you in drag for the first time ever. This is all totally normal and fine.*

"Hey! So, um . . . you survived the car ride with my uncle!" I mentally cringed. *So much for playing it cool.* "I, uh, hope he didn't do anything too embarrassing."

"No, he was great!" Chris said. "We talked about

ceramics and art and stuff. And even J.P. agreed he has great taste in music."

"He's pretty cool," I agreed.

"Definitely," Chris said. An uncomfortable silence settled between us. Chris turned slightly pink. "So, um . . ."

"Yeah," I said, and then it was my turn to blush. "So . . . I, um . . . I do drag."

"I got that," he laughed. "You're really good!"

"You think?"

"Yeah!" he said. "I mean, I don't know much about drag, but as far as I'm concerned, you were robbed."

"Thanks," I said with a small smile. Then I cleared my throat. "Listen, I know I should have told you. We're, like, friends, and stuff, or at least I think we are, and I should have been honest." I looked up at him and held his gaze. "I was just super afraid that you'd think I was weird for doing it, and . . . I didn't want to lose you."

"Lose me?" He wrinkled his nose, then started to laugh. "Martin, no, no way." He reached out and touched my shoulders with his warm, strong hands. "I . . . like you a lot. I want to keep hanging out with you, because . . . you're not like anyone I've ever met before."

"Really?"

"Really," he said. "Hey, I was thinking. What

would you say to video games at my place this weekend?"

"It's a date!" Then I panicked, realizing what I had said. "I mean—"

"It's a date," Chris repeated, his blue eyes sparkling.

And the butterflies shimmied for joy.

I heard a screech from behind me, and suddenly Mom swept in between us. "Mijo!" she cried, throwing her arms out to hug me tight. "Oh, baby, you were wonderful!"

"Mom—I—thanks—I'm—I can't breathe!" I said into her shoulder. She reluctantly let me go, wiping tears from her eyes.

"Couldn't have done it better myself, león," Tío Billy said, his eyes misty. He cleared his throat and threw me our secret handshake.

"You should be very, very proud of yourself," Mom sniffled when we were done.

"She's right," Tío Billy said. "How do you feel?"

How do I feel? I felt like fireworks and snowball fights and the perfect shade of lipstick. I felt like a million solar systems bursting brightly into existence, lighting up the furthest reaches of the universe. I felt incandescent.

"Fierce," I said finally, smiling. "I feel fierce."

★ ★ ★

Above Hoosier Mama, the evening sky glittered like Lottie's gown. After the show, all of us headed out to the parking lot together, drag queens and middle schoolers and grown-ups alike. I took a deep breath of cool night air and closed my eyes.

Somewhere out there is a universe where things are different, I thought. In that universe, Lottie didn't exist. In that universe, Dad had stayed, and Mom never had Tío Billy come to visit. In that universe, I never found my voice.

Maybe I would have liked it there, in that universe. But I would never know for sure—and that was just fine by me. For the first time, I wanted to stay in *my* universe: a universe full of glitter and laughter and love. A universe where I could be me, quiet or loud or somewhere in between.

As we approached the bus, I caught a glimpse of myself in the window, illuminated by moonlight. Carmen and Pickle appeared next to me, then Mom and Tío Billy. In the constellation we formed, Lottie and my family and me, I saw myself, exactly as I wanted to be.

"So, león, what do you think?" Tío Billy asked, turning to me. "You up for another All-Ages Night/ Regionals double-header again next year?"

"Are you kidding?" I smiled. "I could do it backward. And in heels."

ACKNOWLEDGMENTS

Whenever I've been asked "How's book stuff?" in the roughly two-and-a-half years between sitting down to write *Martin* and the first copies hitting shelves, I've responded with slightly manic laughter.

It's the laugh of someone who is 100 percent certain that, any moment now, someone will sneak up behind her, pull off her trench coat, and reveal the roughly seven raccoons playing at authorhood beneath. It's the laugh of someone who literally cannot believe what's happening to her.

How did I get this lucky? It's completely ludicrous! I'm laughing in disbelief as I write this! I've won the great Word Nerd Lottery! Ha-ha!

Utter incredulity aside: Just as Martin relied on his friends, family, and team to help him on the way to his dream, I am ridiculously privileged to have been supported by some of the best humans on the planet. Here come the thank-yous:

First and foremost, to my brilliant agent, Jessica Mileo. You changed the course of my life forever with your vision and stalwart support. I could not have asked for a better champion for this book. Thank you for taking a chance on me; you are a wish upon a shooting star come true.

To my intrepid editor, Rachael Stein. This book is immeasurably better because of your masterful guidance. Thank you for imagining a world with Martin in it, for being my conscience whenever I considered adding another em dash, and for calling me out on just how often I use the word "just."

To the Sterling team, including but not limited to: Theresa Thompson, Hannah Reich, Irene Vandervoort, Lauren Tambini, Blanca Oliviery, Maha Khalil, Chris Vaccari, and Kerry Henderson, as well as freelancers Gina Horowitz and Kimberly Broderick.

To Risa Rodil, *Martin*'s fabulous cover artist. I'm pretty sure it's illegal for any one person to be that talented, but don't worry, your secret is safe with me.

To Anthony LaSasso, publicist and friend. Thank you for holding my hand through my brave new world of author events and for laughing at my bad jokes.

To Silvia Mileo, for giving authenticity to Martin's, Gena's, and Billy's voices. You went above and beyond the call of Literary Agent Mom Duty—eres increíble, Silvia; muchas gracias.

To Verenice Romero Ponce for your knowledge of the Spanish language and all things Celia Cruz.

To Will Harrell, a.k.a. Candy Samples, the very first drag queen to read this book. Thank you for honoring me with your time and expertise!

To Melissa Francis, Lara Ameen, Melissa Blake, and Lili Hadsell for lending their expert perspectives to this book. Your firsthand knowledge helped to better the representation in *Martin*, and I could not be more grateful.

To the LGBTQIA+ community at large, and to drag performers the world over. This book is a love letter to you, your immense strength, your wondrously made hearts, your vital stories. Simply by living your truth, you inspire me to do the same. I am humbled to stand with you.

To all the superb teachers who helped shape me along the way, but especially: Mary Ann Laurencell, Joyce Staniszewski, Kathy Hagedorn, Denise Garvey, Carrie Hallman, Leah Coleman, George Fear, Ralph Crecco, Dan Sackett, and Geoff Epperson.

To Emily Monaco and Amelia-Rose Rubin, the most sensational squad. Thank you for always encouraging me to #ResistTheLizard.

To Michael Fraser, because you asked, and to Margie Fraser, because you didn't.

To Pip and Penelope, the coolest cats around.

To Jenny Berg, who supported *Martin* from the very beginning. When I was in the trenches of this book, you were there next to me, cheering me on with your friendship and hilarity (and sometimes wine). Thank you for all of that (but especially the wine).

To Nick, Jake, Cali, and Olivia. I am so proud to be your cousin, and prouder still of who you've all grown up to be. (Your parents are pretty cool too.)

To Papa, who once changed my world by gently suggesting that I didn't have to be good at everything. I wish you could have seen this.

To my grandmother, Alice Zaczek, a lifelong inspiration to me. Thank you for all the stories, for all the sleepovers, and for all the waffles.

To Erik Zaczek, my "little" brother who has grown into a giant of a man, both in stature and character. I am so proud of you, small orange one. It is an immense privilege to be your big sister and friend.

To my mother, Elizabeth Zaczek, a force of nature. Thank you for always insisting I should be writing, even when I swore those days were over. You fought to give me all the happiness the world could offer, and if I could buy you a lifetime supply of fuzzy socks and Chardonnay as recompense, I would, but instead I have only this: Mom, I'm happy. Thank you for everything.

To my father, Robert Zaczek, my hero. The profound gratitude I feel to be your daughter is beyond language itself. I am who I am because of you. Thank you for giving me your sense of humor, your keen mind, your loving heart. I hope your Peanut has made you proud.

To Andrew Fraser, without whom this book would not exist. In loving me, you changed my life. Your stubborn insistence that I could do this—despite all my equally stubborn protestations to the contrary—gave me the confidence to begin. I hope you know how much I appreciate all you do to keep our life together while I figure out how to be a Grown-Up Author Person. I love you most. (It's in a book now; that means it's true—I don't make the rules!)

And finally, to all the young readers who pick up this book and find comfort or laughter within its pages. Books belong to their readers, and *Martin* is and has always been for you. No matter who you are or what your story is, you are capable of marvelous things. You are *all* the reigning queens of my heart. Sparkle on!